QUICKSILVER

QUICKSILVER
BILL PRONZINI

A "Nameless Detective" Mystery

St. Martin's Press
New York

Library of Congress Cataloging in Publication Data
Pronzini, Bill.
   Quicksilver.
   I. Title.
PS3566.R67Q5 1984   813'.54   83-17654
ISBN 0-312-66081-2

First Edition
10 9 8 7 6 5 4 3 2 1

For Ed and Pat Hoch—
good friends in difficult times

QUICKSILVER

One

The loft was about twenty feet square, which made it plenty big enough for an office. The walls were a sort of beige color, the floor was half linoleum and half bare wood, the ceiling was high and had a skylight and a suspended light fixture that looked like an upside-down grappling hook surrounded by clusters of brass testicles. There were two windows in the wall opposite the door, set apart from each other, and another window in the left-hand wall. That was all—no furnishings of any kind, no anteroom or alcove or closet, nothing else to see except for some miscellaneous streaks and blobs of vari-colored paint on the linoleum half of the floor.

Eberhardt said, "Well? What do you think?"

I didn't know what I thought yet; we'd only just walked through the door. Without saying anything, I went over to one of the windows in the far wall. Wonderful downhill view of the back end of the Federal Building—or there would be on a clear day. Now, with early-December rain pelting down and the noonday sky as dark as dusk, that building and the others nearby were blurry shapes with their tops cut off by low scudding clouds. I moved over to the side-wall window. Out there you had an even more wonderful view of the blank brick wall of the building adjacent to this one.

"Well?" Eberhardt said again. He had followed me from window to window and was breathing on my neck. "Not too bad, is it?"

"Not too bad," I admitted, turning.

"It's not Montgomery Street or the Transamerica pyramid, but what the hell. There are worse neighborhoods; O'Farrell Street's not a bad address, not over this close to Van Ness. And the other tenants are pretty respectable—a custom-shirt company below us and a real estate outfit on the first floor. It's better than that office you used to have on Taylor."

I nodded: he was right on all counts.

"It'll look good when we get it fixed up," he said. "Put down some carpeting, put some pictures on the walls, get the furniture moved in. Have our names painted on the window too, maybe. You like that idea?"

"It's an idea," I said. But I didn't like it; it made me think of Spade and Archer, and how things went with them before Spade got mixed up with the black bird. "What's all that paint on the floor?"

"There was an art school in here before," Eberhardt said. "That's how come the skylight; guy who ran the school had it put in at his own expense. He died a couple of months ago. Ran the school by himself, so it died when he did."

"Who told you all that?"

"Sam Crawford, man who owns the building. He's a friend of Cap Turner, down at the Hall; Cap's the one told me about the place being available."

"Uh-huh."

"He's anxious to rent it. Crawford, I mean. He told me he'll take care of the electric bill, no charge to us. All we got to pay is the telephone and the rent."

"So how much does he want?"

"Didn't I tell you?"

He knew damned well he hadn't told me. He hadn't said anything on the phone except that he'd found a place and I should come take a look at it. "No," I said, "you didn't tell me. How much?"

"Eight-fifty."

"*How* much?"

"Including the electric bill, remember—"

"Eight-fifty a month is too steep, Eb."

"For a place this size? And practically downtown? Besides, I told you before, I can cover the rent for a couple of months if it comes to that."

"I don't know . . ."

"We won't find a better deal," he said. "And you admitted

the place isn't bad. You could work here all right, couldn't you?"
"I suppose I could."
"Well then? I say we take it before somebody else does. Go over
to Crawford's office right now and sign the lease. How about it,
paisan?"

His eyes were eager; it was only the second time in the past four
months, since an assassin's bullets had nearly ended his life, that I
had seen some of his old enthusiasm come back. The first time had
been two and a half weeks ago, just before Thanksgiving, when I'd
quit waffling and done what he'd been after me for weeks to do:
agreed to take him into my investigating business as a full partner.

I'd made that decision against my better judgment, and against
the advice of Kerry Wade and a few other people, and I had thought
more than once of backing out of the commitment. Hell, I was
thinking about it again right now. But I had given him my word;
that was as much as I had to give anybody, and it was something
I did not take lightly, especially with a friend as close as Eberhardt.

Still, I had trouble taking this final step, saying, "All right, Eb,
we'll take the place, we'll go sign the lease." The words seemed to
lodge in my throat. Because once I said them, I would lose something that had been mine alone for twenty-three years, something
I had built and that was an extension of me. The partnership would
change it, reshape it into a thing shared, an uncomfortably intimate
thing like a sexless marriage. I felt as if I were standing in front of
an altar on my wedding day. I felt as if I were losing my freedom.

But it no longer mattered how I felt, really, because I was committed, and so I got the words said. And he grinned a little, with relief
as much as anything else, and smacked me on the arm, and for those
few seconds he looked like the old Eberhardt—the one without the
extra gray in his hair, the one I'd known before his wife left, before
he made the mistake that had led to the shooting and to his self-
imposed retirement from the San Francisco cops. The one who once
had cared. The one who might still care again.

So it was worth it after all, taking him in as a partner, giving up
my little chunk of freedom. If it made him happy again, if it made
him care again, then it wasn't really that much of a sacrifice, was it?

No, damn it. It wasn't.

* * * *

Sam Crawford's office was a gaudy two-room suite over on Bush Street, with a gaudy blond secretary to go with it. Crawford himself wasn't gaudy, though. He was fat, he wore a three-piece suit, he smoked fancy cigars in an onyx holder, and he had a diamond ring on the little finger of his right hand that was probably worth enough to feed a starving family of six for a year. He looked like a photograph I had seen once of a Tammany Hall politician.

He drew up the lease, gabbling the whole time, telling us what a terrific deal we were getting. He also told jokes and laughed a lot, because he had money and money made him a very happy man; he was the kind who would laugh at funerals and make comments like, "Poor schmucks—they never had nothing and now they never will." And he volunteered the information that he owned a dozen other buildings around the city, including three in Hunters Point and five in the Fillmore district. But he wasn't a slum landlord, he said. Perish the thought. He gave his people a break whenever he could, damn right he did. That was the phrase he used: "his people," as if he were talking about expensive livestock.

Yeah, I thought, some benefactor. I liked him about as much as I liked potato bugs and rodents with fangs. But then, I would have had trouble liking anybody I met about now. I was feeling blue and a little "gruffly"—Kerry's word to describe that low, snappish mood you get into sometimes, when nothing seems quite right and everything and everybody annoys you. It was a reaction to finalizing the partnership with Eberhardt, of course; I knew that, but I couldn't find a way to bring myself out of it. I had enough trouble trying to control myself so I wouldn't tell Crawford what I thought he ought to do with his three buildings in Hunters Point and his five in the Fillmore.

We signed the lease finally, and Eberhardt wrote a check, and we got out of there. The last thing Crawford said to us was that we could move in any time, he'd only charge us a half-month's rent from the fifteenth; he blew cigar smoke in my face as he said it, making my stomach lurch. So I was doubly glad to get outside into clean air again, even though the rain was coming down in sheets now and the wind howled and moaned and assaulted the cars parked at the curb.

When we reached my car in the next block we were both sodden.

I started the engine and put the heater on high, and we sat there for a time trying to dry off. Pretty soon Eberhardt said, "Crawford's a jerk."

I looked at him. "You noticed, huh?"

"Sure. This morning, the first time I laid eyes on him. But we don't have to deal with him much; he's not the kind of landlord who comes around poking his nose into things. And I still say we lucked out."

"Maybe so."

"How about if we open shop next Monday?" he said. "The State Board's approved my application for a license, so we don't have to wait on that account. And we'll have four days to get the stuff moved in."

"Yeah, okay."

"I'll ring up Ma Bell, make arrangements for the phones. Two, you think?"

"Any more and they'd think we were going to make book."

He laughed. It startled me a little; I couldn't remember the last time I'd heard him laugh. "I'll buy a desk for myself," he said. "From one of those office furniture places on Mission that sells used. Anything else I should get?"

"Suit yourself."

"What outfit did you store your stuff with?"

I told him.

"Can they get it delivered by Monday?"

"I don't see why not. I'll give them a call."

"So then we're just about set."

"Just about."

"Listen," he said seriously, "it's going to work out, you'll see. I'll carry my weight; and I won't try to throw any of it around with you. You're the boss—you tell me what to do and I'll do it."

I didn't say anything. I knew Eberhardt from way back; he was used to being in charge, he was stubborn, he had his own way of doing things and he always thought it was the right way, and on certain issues he was either blind or had tunnel vision. He meant what he said about following orders—at this moment. But later on, when push came to shove on this or that case? I didn't want to think about that, because I was fairly sure I knew how it would go. What I didn't know, and wouldn't until it happened, was how I would handle it.

He got one of his scabrous pipes out of his overcoat pocket and clamped it between his teeth. "I don't know about you," he said around the stem, "but I'm starving. What say we go somewhere and put on the feed bag? Out to the Old Clam House, maybe, get some fried oysters . . ."

Fried oysters, I thought, and my stomach lurched the way it had when Crawford blew his cigar smoke at me. But not for the same reason. "I can't, Eb," I said, not without reluctance.

"Why not? Ah, Christ, you still on that diet?"

"Afraid so."

"You're no fatter than you ever were," he said. "What the hell do you want to lose weight for?"

"My health. It's not good to have a gut like mine at my age."

"You never worried about your gut before. Kerry's behind this diet business, I'll bet."

She was—she'd been after me for months to take off fifteen or twenty pounds—but I didn't want to tell him that. I hadn't told him or anyone else about her abortive attempts to get me to go jogging on a regular basis and I shouldn't have told him about the diet either. He was tall and slender, all angles and blunt planes, and he'd never had a weight problem. He didn't understand the way it was for guys like me.

"Nah," I said, "it's not Kerry's doing, it's mine. I'm tired of having to lift up my belly every time I want to see what I've got hanging underneath."

Eberhardt laughed again. It was a joke at my expense this time, but that was all right. At least it got him off the subject. I had enough trouble with the diet as it was, without talking about it. All that did was make me think about food.

I drove him back to O'Farrell Street, dropped him off at his car, and then went home to my flat in Pacific Heights. There was nothing else to do; I had no work right now. I wished to Christ I did—one more case that I could call my own, one last solo investigative fling. Well, maybe something would turn up today or tomorrow, something simple that I could dispose of before next Monday, without involving Eberhardt.

I had to park the car a block and a half away from my building, and even my underwear was wet by the time I let myself into the foyer. From inside the ground floor apartment that belonged to my friend Litchak, the retired fire inspector, I could smell something cooking. Stew, maybe, or some other Lithuanian dish with lots of garlic in it. My mouth began to water. And my stomach began to ache. All I'd had to eat today was two eggs and an orange for breakfast. For lunch I was supposed to have a green salad and some more eggs. Every day now for ten days, eggs for breakfast and eggs for lunch and sometimes even eggs for supper. Jesus Christ. What kind of food was that for a big, active man? Pretty soon I would start flapping and squawking and pecking the ground like an undernourished chicken.

I went and stripped out of my sodden clothes and got on the bathroom scale. Same reading as this morning and yesterday morning, too: 228 pounds. I had lost exactly two pounds in ten days. I said a nasty word. And then took a hot shower to get myself warm again. That was another thing about dieting; you were cold all the time, because you weren't getting enough fuel to stoke the furnace.

My stomach kept growling. I didn't want the eggs, I was beginning to hate eggs, but I was so hungry I could have eaten the carton. I couldn't even fry the damn things, oh no, because there were too many calories in butter and margarine and oil; I had to softboil them. So I put water on and made a salad out of lettuce and cucumbers; no dressing, too many calories in dressing, just a little vinegar and some salt and pepper. I ate the salad while I waited for the water to boil. Rabbit food. Rabbits and chickens. Bah!

After I started the eggs cooking I went back into the bedroom and checked my answering machine. Two calls. The first one made me cringe a little; it was from Jeanne Emerson and she said she was back in town and wanted to know when we could get together to do our article. The article was supposed to be all about me and my career and the trials and tribulations I'd had in recent months; Jeanne was a photojournalist. She thought I represented "the common man's struggle to maintain his ideals while working within a restrictive system." Which was something of a crock as far as I was concerned, but she was pretty serious about it.

She was also pretty serious about *me*. Back in October, she'd kept calling and hinting around about us seeing more of each other, and it had made me uncomfortable. I wouldn't have minded seeing *all* of her if she'd come into my life more than eight months ago, because she was a very good-looking Chinese lady; but as it was, I had my hands and my heart full of another very good-looking lady, Kerry Wade, who had come into my life exactly eight months ago. I didn't want to do anything stupid to jeopardize my relationship with Kerry. So it had been a distinct relief when Jeanne picked up a lucrative magazine assignment and went off to the wilds of Mexico for six weeks.

Only now my reprieve had ended and here she was again, and I still didn't know how to handle the situation. Do the article and run the risk of succumbing to temptation. Don't do the article and offend Jeanne and lose some free publicity. Terrific choice. I needed more time to think about it. So I wouldn't return her call right away, I decided. For all she knew, I might be out of town myself.

Some tough, brave private eye I was. Mix me up with a woman or two and I came apart like cardboard in a rainstorm.

The other call on the machine, coincidentally, was also from an Oriental woman—a Japanese this time, who said her name was Haruko Gage and that she needed the services of an investigator. That perked me up a little; maybe it was the job I'd been lusting after. I wrote down her number, then went back into the kitchen to rescue my eggs. I put them on a plate and looked at them for about ten seconds. Then I opened the refrigerator and got out a celery stalk and put that on top of the salad in my grumbling stomach. I wasn't *eating* these days; I was either swallowing chicken fruit or grazing like a bloody horse.

Kerry, I thought, the things I do for you.

In the bedroom again, I dialed Haruko Gage's number. A man answered, and when I asked for the lady he wanted to know who was calling; he sounded timid and wary. I told him. "Oh, right," he said, and the wariness was gone and he sounded timid and unhappy. "Well, she had to go out for a few minutes, but she'll be back before long. I'm her husband. Art Gage?" He made his name into a question, as if he wasn't sure who he was.

"What is it your wife wants to see me about, Mr. Gage?"

"These presents she keeps getting."

"Presents?"

"In the mail. It's driving us crazy."

"What sort of presents are you talking about?"

Pause. "I guess I'd better let Haruko tell you. It was her idea to hire a private detective."

"All right. I'll call back a little later, then—"

"No, no," he said, "why don't you just come over to the house? She'll be back by the time you get here."

"Where do you live, Mr. Gage?"

"On Buchanan, just off Bush." He gave me the number. "It's on the fringe of Japantown."

The address was only about ten minutes from my flat. I looked out through the bedroom window to see if it was still raining so hard. It wasn't, so I said, "I think I've got time to stop by. Give me about half an hour."

"I'll tell Haruko you're coming."

We rang off, and I put some dry clothes on and combed my hair. Then I called the outfit where my office stuff was stored and made arrangements for them to deliver it to O'Farrell Street tomorrow afternoon. And then I went back into the kitchen to eat those goddamn eggs.

Two

Japantown was just off Geary Boulevard in the Western Addition, a few minutes from downtown—a miniature *ginza* where a high percentage of San Francisco's 11,000 citizens of Japanese descent lived and worked, and where a good many Nippon tourists either stayed or congregated. Its hub, the Japan Center, was a five-acre complex built in 1968 that housed restaurants, a large hotel, a theatre, Japanese baths, art galleries, bookstores, banks, plenty of shops, and a pedestrian mall that was supposed to look like a mountain village in the old country, complete with a meandering stream, plum and cherry trees, and fountains. On the dozen or so other blocks of Japantown, you found small businesses, hotels, a bowling alley, a couple of Japanese-language newspapers, apartment houses, and not a few old—and for the most part refurbished—stick-style Victorian houses.

But the area surrounding the *Nihonmachi* wasn't anywhere near as pleasant. There were a lot of low-income housing projects, and a lot of anger and frustration to go with them; Japantown and its residents and visitors were prime targets for young hoodlums. Security measures had been taken and police patrols increased, but it was still one of the city's high-crime districts. That was a damned shame for several reasons, not the least of which was the fact that the Japanese were a polite, friendly, and law-abiding people. They could have given lessons to too many of the white and black population.

There wasn't much doing in Japantown this afternoon because of the weather. Street parking was usually at a premium, even up around Bush and Buchanan, but I found a place half a dozen doors down from the address Art Gage had given me. That block of Buchanan was quiet, tree-shaded, flanked by well-kept Victorians painted in bright colors in the modern fashion. The Gage house was one of an identically restored group, like a row of architectural clones: light blue walls and stoop, dark blue trim, with accents in red and gold.

I hustled up onto the narrow porch, shook rainwater off my hat, and rang the bell. The door opened pretty soon and I was looking at a slender, almost fragile blondish guy of about thirty. He was handsome in an undistinguished sort of way, or he would have been if he hadn't had a weak chin, liquidy blue eyes, and the too-white skin of a shut-in. He was wearing Levi's, moccasins, and a blue Pendleton shirt.

He said, "You're the detective?"

"Yes."

"Come on in. Haruko's in the front room."

He took my coat and hat, then led me down a short hall and through an archway into 1920. Chairs with tufted velvet cushions, little round tables with fringed gold cloths, rococo lighting fixtures, a tiled Queen Anne fireplace above which were mirrored glass panels. There was too much furniture: china cabinets and a highboy and a secretary desk and a claw-footed mahogany couch, in addition to all the chairs and tables. It had the look of a room designed for show rather than comfort, like a private museum exhibit. But the problem was, none of the furnishings appeared to be a genuine antique; even I could tell that. They were an oddball mixture of reproductions, simulations, and garage-sale junk.

The woman sitting on the claw-footed couch looked out of place among all that ersatz Victorian stuff. She was in her mid-twenties, not much over five feet tall, small-boned, inclining to plumpness, with classically pretty Japanese features and silky black hair that would hang to her waist when she was standing. But there was none of the delicacy that you usually found in small Oriental women. I sensed instead a willful strength, a kind of sharp-edged Occidental determination. If appearances were accurate, there wasn't much doubt as to who ran the Gage household.

She stood up as her husband and I crossed the room. Gage performed the introductions, and she gave me her hand and a small solemn smile. "Thank you for coming," she said. "I'm sorry I wasn't here when you called back; I had to deliver some designs to one of our customers."

"Designs?"

"We're artistic designers," Gage said. "And creative consultants for several large firms—"

She looked at him and said, "Art," and he shut up. Then she said to me, "My husband likes to glorify what we do. The truth is, we design wallpaper."

"Ah," I said, a little blankly.

She laughed. "It's one of those odd professions most people aren't aware of. They look at wallpaper, even the most intricately patterned kind, and they take it for granted; they don't realize someone has to have designed it."

"It's not simple work, either," Gage said. He sounded defensive. "It takes a lot of talent, you know."

"I'm sure it does, Mr. Gage."

"Besides, it pays very well—"

"Art," she said.

He quit talking again and took a package of cigarettes out of his shirt pocket and set about getting one lighted. He didn't look at either his wife or me while he did it.

She asked me, "Would you like some tea? I'm going to have a cup."

"Well . . . I'd prefer coffee if you have it."

"Of course. Art, will you put the water on? Make my tea the lemon grass, all right?"

He gave her a look like a housewife reacting to a bossy husband. But he didn't say anything. And he went out of the room almost immediately, the cigarette hanging out of his face.

Haruko sat on the couch again. I sat on one of the fake Victorian chairs; it was about as comfortable as sitting on a fence. The rain made a steady thrumming noise beyond the room's velveteen-draped bay windows. Out in the kitchen, Gage banged pots and cupboard doors—angry sounds in the stillness.

I said, "What was it you wanted to see me about, Mrs. Gage? Your husband mentioned something about presents, but he didn't elaborate."

"I'm glad he didn't. He gets emotional on the subject."

"What sort of presents are they?"

"Expensive ones. Different pieces of jewelry. The latest was a white jade ring."

"Who's sending them to you?"

"I don't know," she said.

I raised an eyebrow.

"That's the problem," she said. "That's why I want to hire you —to find out who's doing it."

"Let me get this straight. These gifts come in the mail?"

"Yes. First-class."

"No return address?"

"None."

"Insured?"

"No."

"Postmarked where?"

"Here in the city—all of them."

"No accompanying notes or anything?"

"Only with the first one. A one-line note."

"What did it say?"

"It said, 'With all the love in my heart.' "

"Just that?"

"Yes."

"Do you still have the note?"

She nodded. "I saved it and the wrappings from the last couple of packages. I'll have Art get them for you. The jewelry, too."

"When did the first package arrive?"

"A little over two months ago."

"How many others have there been?"

"Three. One last Saturday, another yesterday."

"And you say they all contained expensive jewelry?"

"Yes. Four pieces, each one different, worth a total of over eight thousand dollars. I had them appraised."

"That's a lot of money for anonymous gifts."

"Exactly," she said.

"And you have no idea at all who's sending them?"

"None. It's driving Art crazy. He thinks I either had or am having an affair." She gave me a level look. "He's wrong. If they were that sort of present I certainly wouldn't have told him about them, would I?"

"I don't suppose you would."

"Art is like a little boy sometimes," she said, and the tone of her voice indicated she felt that was pretty much true of all men. I decided I would not have liked being married to her. But then, I wouldn't be her type anyhow. Art Gage was her type; I had a feeling she hadn't picked him by accident.

I said, "Is your husband's jealousy the reason you decided to hire a private detective?"

"Not really. At first the presents were amusing; every woman likes the idea of a secret admirer. But now I'm getting worried. Whoever he is, he has to be at least a little crazy. Who knows what he might do?"

I made an agreeing noise: she was right.

"I want to know who he is," she said, "and I want him to stop sending me things. And I don't want him bothering me in any other way."

"*Has* he bothered you in any other way? Anonymous phone calls, cars following you, anything like that?"

"No. Just the gifts. I'll even give the jewelry back to him if that's what it takes."

"You mean you'd prefer to keep it?"

"Of course. Why shouldn't I?"

I just looked at her.

"Well," she said, "he's put me through all this worry. And now there's the expense of hiring a detective. Don't let this house fool you; Art's dad is a realtor and he got it for us cheap and gave us part of the down payment as a wedding present. We aren't all that well off. Designing wallpaper makes us a good living, but there's no extra money for luxury items. And I like nice things. What woman doesn't?"

Neat rationalizations. But I was not going to argue with her; what she did with the jewelry was her business, not mine.

"Your admirer is probably somebody you know," I said. "It usually works that way. Do you have many male friends?"

"Not many, no. Mutual friends of Art's and mine, mostly. But none of them has eight thousand dollars to spend on fancy jewelry. Besides, they're all perfectly normal guys."

Sure, I thought. Except that nobody knows what goes on inside another person's head. Any number of "perfectly normal" people have committed all sorts of screwball acts, from mass murder on down to indecent exposure in front of old ladies, zoo animals, and park statues.

I asked, "How long have you been married, Mrs. Gage?"

"A little over two years."

"Your first marriage?"

"Yes."

"Any serious involvements prior to that?"

"Well . . . I dated a lot of men."

"Did any of them ever propose marriage?"

"Yes. One."

"So *he* must have been pretty serious, then."

"I suppose he was."

"How did he take it when you turned him down?"

"He was disappointed, naturally." She frowned; you could see her working her memory. "Very disappointed, as a matter of fact. But I can't imagine . . . no, it couldn't be Kinji. He's only been in this country six years and his beliefs are old-world."

"How do you mean?"

"His beliefs toward women. They're very proper."

"You said his name is Kinji?"

"Kinji Shimata. He owns an art gallery at the Japan Center."

"Successful, this gallery?"

"Oh yes. He could have afforded all that jewelry, but I still can't—"

A sudden shrill whistling interrupted her: a tea kettle going off in the kitchen. The noise went on for four or five seconds, until Art Gage did something about it. I used the time to get out my notebook and write down Kinji Shimata's name.

"Were there any other men serious about you?" I asked Haruko.

"Well, Nelson Mixer asked me to move in with him. But that was purely sexual, I think. It's not the same as a serious proposal of marriage."

"Maybe not," I said, but I was thinking that it could be. "This Mixer is Caucasian, I take it?"

"Yes. He teaches California and U.S. history at City College. I met him there while I was taking some classes three years ago."

"Have you had any contact with him since your marriage?"

"No. I haven't seen Nelson since right after I refused to move in with him. I haven't been back to City College and we don't move in the same circles."

"So Mixer went away quietly, then—no bad feelings or anything like that?"

"No. Nelson isn't that kind."

"What about Kinji Shimata? Did *he* go away quietly?"

"Yes. I still see him now and then, because the Japan Center is so close. He's always very polite and reserved."

Art Gage reappeared carrying a lacquered-wood tray with two cups and little bowls of sugar and milk on it. He put the tray on a boxy-looking table between his wife and me. Then, without saying anything, he went over and sat down next to her.

She let him get settled before she said, "Art, would you get the jewelry and the other stuff and bring it down? The jewelry's in the bedroom; the rest is in that box in the studio."

He gave her an irritated look; she gave it right back to him. It was no contest. His will was about as strong as an old lady's belch, and hers was like pig-iron; he'd never be able to hold out against her for more than a few minutes on the best day he ever had. This wasn't his best day and he didn't make it past five seconds. He sighed and said, "Shit," and got up and went out of the room again.

"Any other men you dated more than casually?" I asked Haruko. "Who might care for you more than you thought at the time?"

"The only one I can think of is Edgar Ogada." She hesitated, then reached for her tea and said, "And Ken Yamasaki, I suppose. I never did know what he was thinking."

"Let's take this Ken Yamasaki first. Who's he?"

"Just a guy I went out with for a while. He works evenings—I guess he still does—at Tamura's Baths. That's a Japanese bathhouse on Pine Street."

"So he isn't well off financially, then."

"Because he works in a bathhouse? Well, I'm not sure. His family must have money; he always had plenty of it to spend."

I did some scribbling in my notebook. "What did you mean, you never knew what he was thinking?"

"Oh, Ken is very quiet and introspective. He reads a lot—Albert Camus, for one, if you can imagine a Japanese-American reading Camus."

I couldn't imagine it because I had no idea who Albert Camoo was. Some French writer? Well, it didn't matter; I probably wouldn't have liked his work anyway. Pulp writers were the ones I liked, which no doubt made me a lowbrow and a cretin in some people's eyes. But that didn't matter either. As far as I was concerned, lowbrows and cretins had snobs beat all to hell.

"How long did you date Yamasaki?" I asked.

"Off and on for a few months."

"When was that?"

"About two and a half years ago."

"Have you seen much of him since?"

"No. I've run into him a couple of times, the last one at a festival a few months ago. That was the last time I saw Edgar, too, come to think of it. He was there with his father."

"Edgar Ogada, you mean?"

"Yes. He's the only old boyfriend I still get together with once in a while."

"Tell me about him."

"Well, I guess you could say Edgar's a free spirit. All he's interested in is having a good time: parties, sports car races, sailing, that kind of thing. I liked him a lot when I first met him five years ago —I still do—but I could never have gotten deeply involved with him. He has no ambition, so he'll never be successful at anything."

Uh-huh, I thought. Meaning you couldn't manipulate him the way you do Artie.

"I think he still loves me in his own way," she said. "That's why I mentioned him. But he just couldn't be my admirer. He isn't the type to send anonymous presents; it isn't his style."

"Could he afford to spend the money?"

"I'm not sure. Maybe he could."

"What does he do for a living?"

"He works for his father. The Ogada Nursery on El Camino, in South San Francisco."

"Is that the plant kind of nursery?"

"Yes."

I wrote Edgar Ogada's name and address in the notebook. Then I tried some of my coffee; it was weak and tepid. Yeah, that figured, since Art Gage had made it. I was putting the cup down again when Gage came clomping back into the room. In one hand was a smallish cardboard box; in the other were four little jewelry cases. He put everything on the table next to the lacquered tray and plunked himself down next to Haruko again. She didn't look at him and neither did I.

One of the items in the cardboard box was a sheet of ruled notepaper that had been folded several times. The words on it— *With all the love in my heart*—had been written in ink, the fountain pen variety, in a crabbed, almost childlike scrawl.

I looked up at Haruko. "The printing on this isn't at all familiar to you?"

"No."

"Do you know anyone who still uses a fountain pen?"

"I can't think of anyone, no."

I picked up one of the package wrappings. Haruko's name and address had been printed in the same crabbed scrawl. Someone trying to disguise his handwriting? Maybe. The wrapping didn't tell me anything else. Plain brown paper, the kind you can buy in any dime store. Stamps affixed in neat rows. No return address, no other markings.

The jewelry cases were plain, without any sort of store identification. The four pieces they contained—the white jade ring, a gold locket shaped like a heart with a pearl inlaid on the front, a diamond pendant, and a pair of sapphire earrings—were each free of inscriptions or traceable markings. The jade ring was bulky, more a man's type than a woman's, and it had some tiny scratches on it, as if it might not be new. I found a scratch on the locket, too. But the earrings and the pendant appeared never to have been worn.

"There isn't much here to go on, really," I said. "I'll investigate for you, Mrs. Gage, but I can't promise you anything more than an honest effort. A case like this, where you're dealing with anonymous mailings . . . well, it all depends on who's responsible. If it's one of the men you mentioned, there's a fairly good chance I can either find out or at least intimidate him enough by my presence so that he quits pestering you. If it isn't one of those men, if it's someone you know only casually, for instance, there's just not much I can do."

Haruko nodded. "I understand. I considered all that before I decided to call you."

Gage said, "Listen, hon, I'm not so sure about this—"

"Art."

"Well, I'm *not* sure it's a good idea," he said. He switched his gaze to me. "How much do you charge?"

"Two hundred dollars a day, plus expenses."

"My God! Haruko . . . Christ, we can't afford—"

"Art," she said sharply, "be quiet. We can afford it; the value of the jewelry more than covers the expense. It's something that has to be done."

Gage didn't like it, but he did shut up again. He sat there looking petulant.

"I'll hire you for three days," Haruko said to me. "That should be enough time for you to ask questions and see if you're getting anywhere, shouldn't it?"

"It should be, yes."

"If you find out something and need more time, we can talk about that later. Will you start right away?"

"Yes. I'll do what I can today and make up the rest of the time on Sunday."

"How much of an advance do you want?"

"A hundred dollars would be fine."

She didn't make Gage fetch the family checkbook; she actually got off the couch and went to the secretary desk herself. She had nice hips, if you like them plump. Gage obviously did; he watched her move with low heat in his eyes. While she was writing the check I got out the standard contract form I'd brought with me and filled it in. I had Haruko sign it, then handed her a copy in exchange for the check.

Gage got off his tail, and the two of them accompanied me to the door. As I was putting on my coat and hat, and telling Haruko I'd check in with her sometime tomorrow at the latest, Gage draped a tentative arm around her shoulders. She didn't shrug him off; instead she nuzzled against him, all kittenish now that she'd got her way, and slid her own arm about his waist. He lost his petulant look, gave me a fatuous grin over the top of her head.

Love, I thought. Ain't it wonderful?

I got out of there.

Three

The Shimata Gallery was in the west wing of the Japan Center, sandwiched between a bookstore and a shop that sold Japanese dolls and puppets. It was a smallish place, with a lot of open floor space and most of its merchandise displayed on table-sized, clear plastic cubes. When I walked in, the only other people there were a dignified-looking Japanese guy of about thirty-five and a scrawny dowager type who had a toy poodle tucked under one arm. They were having a conversation about something called a *Noh* mask from the seventeenth century; evidently the dowager wanted to give it to her husband for Christmas and was worried that it wouldn't arrive from Japan in time.

I wandered around looking at the artwork on display, waiting for them to get done with their business. Handpainted screens, woodblock prints and carvings, scroll paintings, a huge samurai sword in an ornamental scabbard. And a lot of delicate porcelain enameled in whites, reds, blues, and golds: vases, boxes, candlesticks, teapots, beakers, cups and saucers. Some of the stuff appeared to be antique and all of it appeared to be expensive. Proof of that was the absence of any price tags.

On the way over from the Gage house—I'd walked because it was only two blocks and the rain had stopped for a while—I had tried to decide on the best way to handle this job. I was still deciding. It was one of those oddballs that come along now and then: no crime had been committed, not even a misdemeanor; technically, whoever had sent the presents to Haruko Gage wasn't even guilty of harassment. So normal investigative channels weren't going to be of any use. And I had to be careful not to say or do anything that could get anybody after *me* for harrassment. About the only tack I could see to take was the straightforward one—be upfront about who I was and what I was doing, see how things developed with each of the people I talked to, and let instinct guide me the rest of the way.

It figured to be routine and pretty dull work; nothing stimulating, nothing that called for deduction or fancy footwork. Just flatfoot stuff—a lot of running around and interviewing. But that was okay. You couldn't always get challenging cases; and the pulp private eyes could have the exotic ones that involved slinky blondes and guys with guns. All I really wanted anyway was something to occupy my mind for the next few days, so I could keep it off Jeanne Emerson, my diet, Eberhardt, and the new joint office.

It took five minutes for the dignified-looking Japanese to convince the dowager that her *Noh* mask would "most definitely" be in her hands by the twentieth of the month. She didn't look at me as she went out, but the toy poodle gave me a baleful glare. I glared back at it, thinking: The hell with you too, pooch.

The Japanese guy came over to where I was standing in front of one of the display cubes. There was an air of reserve about him, but it wasn't the snooty kind. He wore a three-piece suit, charcoal black, with a maroon-and-silver tie. He had a mouth so thin and straight that it might have been drawn on with a ruler and a flesh-colored marking pen, and over his eyes were a pair of tinted Mr. Moto glasses. The glasses looked better on him than they ever had on Peter Lorre.

"*Konnichiwa,*" he said politely. "Good afternoon."

"Good afternoon. Mr. Shimata? Kinji Shimata?"

He bowed. "How may I help you, sir?"

I told him my name and what I did for a living. Nothing changed in his expression then, and nothing changed in it when I said, "I'm conducting an investigation on behalf of Mrs. Haruko Gage."

"Yes?" he said.

"You know Mrs. Gage, of course."

"I am acquainted with her. Why is it she would need a private detective?"

"Somebody's been bothering her," I said.

"Bothering?"

"Sending her anonymous presents in the mail. Expensive presents, one with a love note included."

Five seconds of silence went by. Then he said, "Does she believe I am responsible?" His voice sounded a little stiffer than it had before, but that was all. Behind the Mr. Moto glasses, his eyes were about as emotionally expressive as a carp's.

"No," I said, "she doesn't have any idea who's responsible. I'm trying to find out." I paused. "Whoever the man is, he's probably someone she knows."

"I see."

"And he has money—quite a bit of it."

"Ah?"

"The presents are all pieces of valuable jewelry."

"I do not sell jewelry," Shimata said. "Or give it as a gift."

"Any idea who might want to give it as a gift?"

"None whatever."

"It's pretty obvious that the man's in love with her," I said. "You were in love with her once, weren't you, Mr. Shimata?"

"Ah. She told you I once proposed marriage."

"She did."

"A mistake," he said. "A grave mistake. She did not do me the honor of accepting; for this, I am now grateful."

"Why is that?"

"She would not have made me a good wife."

"No? Why not?"

"She is a demanding woman. A materialist. I am surprised she wishes no more of this expensive jewelry."

"She's worried the admirer might want something in return one of these days."

"Ah. Yes, I understand."

I wasn't getting anywhere with him. His voice revealed nothing more than his words, and his eyes still resembled a carp's. If there was any hot and unrequited passion for Haruko Gage burning inside him, he had it buried deep and under control, at least as far as outward appearances were concerned.

I said, "Well, I won't keep you any longer, Mr. Shimata. I appreciate your talking to me."

"Not at all." He bowed slightly. *"Sayonara."*

"Sure—*sayonara.*"

So much for Kinji Shimata. One down, three to go.

On the Buchanan Mall across the street I found a public telephone kiosk and looked up the address and telephone number of Tamura's Baths. The bathhouse was only about six blocks from here, just outside the unofficial boundary of Japantown. I wrote the numbers down in my notebook, then put a dime in the coin slot and rang the place up.

The woman who answered told me in a thick Japanese accent that Ken Yamasaki didn't come to work until six o'clock. I asked for his address, but she wouldn't give it to me. So I thanked her, broke the connection, and looked up his name in the directory. That didn't do me any good either; there were seven Yamasaki's listed, none of whom was named Ken or Kenneth.

I flipped back to the *M*'s. Nelson Mixer *was* listed—an address out on 46th Avenue—but when I dialed his number nobody answered. My watch said it was quarter of four; there was still a chance I could catch him on campus at the city college.

It took me twenty minutes to drive out to where CCSF was located on Phelan Avenue off Ocean. It was a good-sized complex, built on hilly terrain, with a domed science building and its own fieldhouse and football and track stadium. A bunch of students were milling around under umbrellas in front of the campus bookstore; I asked one of them where the registrar's office was. He told me— Colan Hall—and pointed it out, and I got myself rained on pretty good before I got there.

I also got rained on inside, figuratively speaking. "I'm sorry, sir," the woman at the registrar's desk said. "Professor Mixer isn't teaching today. He's ill."

"I'm sorry to hear that."

"Yes, sir. He has the flu. We've had a large number of absentees because of it—the weather, you know."

"Uh-huh. Will he be in tomorrow, do you think?"

"I really couldn't say."

So I left her and got a little wetter on my way back to the car. Now what? I could drive all the way across town to Mixer's residence, but I decided against it. He hadn't answered the phone earlier, which meant he either wasn't home or he was too ill to get out of bed. Either way, I would probably be wasting my time.

Nelson Mixer, I thought as I started the engine. What the hell kind of name was that, anyway? It didn't sound like a man; it sounded like a brand of quinine water.

When I located the Ogada Nursery in South San Francisco it was almost five o'clock and fully dark. My headlights picked up the rain-washed sign first, mounted at the edge of a muddy private road that branched off El Camino Real—WHOLE-SALE ONLY the sign said—and then the buildings and some open fields beyond. There were two long rows of attached greenhouses made out of corrugated, opaque fiberglass sheets, half a dozen in each row, with the rows set at right angles to each other. In the ell between them was a smaller wooden structure that might have been a potting shed. Off to one side, where the road ended,

was a modest white frame house with some cypress shrubbery surrounding it.

There weren't any lights on in the greenhouses or in the frame
house, but the windows of the smaller wooden building shone a
misty yellow through the rain. I parked on a blacktopped area under
the overhang of the shed's roof, next to an old pickup truck with a
bashed-in front fender and broken headlight. I got out and ran over
and whacked on the door with my hand.

It opened after about ten seconds, revealing a short, stoop-shoul-
dered Japanese of indeterminate middle-age. His black hair was shot
through with streaks of white, but the skin of his face and hands was
mostly free of wrinkles. He looked tired, as if he'd been working long
hours without much rest. He had a trowel in one hand; bits of soil
and mulch clung to the fingers of the other.

"Yes, please?" he said.

"I'm looking for Mr. Ogada—"

"I am Mr. Ogada."

"No, sir, I mean Edgar Ogada. Your son?"

"Yes, Edgar is my son. But he isn't here."

"When do you expect him back?"

He shrugged. "Tonight. Tomorrow he must deliver all of these."
He opened the door a little wider and gestured with the trowel. It
was a potting shed, all right, among other things, and right now it
was jammed with Christmas poinsetta plants; they were lined up in
rows on several benches and on the floor.

"But you don't know what time tonight he'll be back?" I asked.

"No, I'm sorry."

"Or where I might find him?"

"No. Edgar comes and goes as he pleases. You are a friend of his?"

"We've never met. I have a small personal matter to discuss with
him."

"Come back tomorrow afternoon," Mr. Ogada said. "After
twelve o'clock. The poinsettas will be delivered by then."

"Thanks. I'll do that."

He shut the door and I ran back to the car. So far I had not
accomplished much in the way of earning my fee; I hadn't even been
able to track down Yamasaki, Mixer, or Edgar Ogada yet. What with
the rain and the hunger pains that were starting up again in my

stomach, not to mention Eberhardt and the new office, it had not been an all-star day.

But there was still time to salvage it. I could talk to Ken Yamasaki later tonight, for one thing. And much more important than that, I was going to spend the evening with Kerry. The whole night with her, maybe.

Like the song says: Who could ask for anything more?

Four

Kerry was reading a pulp magazine when I got to her apartment on Diamond Heights. She had it open in her hand as she let me in —an early forties issue of *Midnight Detective,* one of a batch I had loaned her at her request. I recognized it from the garish cover painting of two Caucasian guys getting ready to blow up an Oriental in a mandarin robe; they had two sticks of dynamite apiece and the Oriental had a hatchet in one long-nailed claw and a big automatic in the other, and there was a half-naked girl lying on the ground to one side, tied up and looking terrified. It was a typical pulp cover: none of it made much sense.

She shut the door, gave me a quick kiss, and started to poke her nose back into the magazine. I said, "Is that all I get?"

"For now."

"Must be a pretty interesting story you're reading."

"It is. One of Russ Dancer's."

"Good old Russ."

"Mmm. I'll be done in a minute; I only have two more pages to go." She turned back toward the living room.

"I think I'll have a beer," I said casually.

"No you won't," she said. "There's diet soda in the fridge. Tab and Fresca."

Tab and Fresca, I thought. Fifty-four years old, I come in from a hard day on the job, and what am I supposed to drink? Crap with

saccharine in it that had croaked a lot of laboratory animals. Tab and
Fresca. Bah.

Instead of making for the kitchen, I followed Kerry into the living
room and watched her curl up on her modernistic couch with the
copy of *Midnight Detective*. She was nice to watch—anytime, anywhere, no matter what she was doing. Tall, willowy without being
skinny, terrific legs, and a fanny to start a monk drooling into his
cowl. Shoulder-length auburn hair; dark green chameleon eyes that
changed shades according to her moods; humor lines crinkled
around the eyes and a wide, soft mouth. Fifteen years younger than
me, a fact which upset the hell out of her father, an ex-pulp writer
called—by me, anyway—Ivan the Terrible. The thought of old Ivan
being upset made me smile. I liked Ivan about as much as I liked
being on a diet.

As for Kerry—hell, I *loved* her and I didn't care who knew it.

She finished the story pretty soon and put the magazine down.
"That," she said, "was pure hokum. But I loved every word of it."

I couldn't remember which of Dancer's stories was in that issue.
I asked, "One of the Rex Hannigans?"

"No. Straight suspense, not a private eye story. All about midgets
and burial crypts and a four-foot headless ghost that really isn't a
ghost at all."

"Oh, yeah, that one. What was it called?"

" 'No Head for My Short Bier.' "

"Uh-huh. Inspired titles back then."

"Dumb titles, you mean. The writing's good, though. Dancer was
a craftsman in those days."

"He was," I said, and let it go at that. Dancer had, since the
demise of the pulps in the early fifties, turned into a hack writer of
paperback originals and a full-fledged alcoholic. One of the reasons
was Kerry's mother, Cybil, who was also an ex-pulp writer; Dancer
had been in love with her back in the forties and had never gotten
over it. I'd found that out during a pulp convention earlier in the
year that had reunited the Wades and Dancer and a bunch of other
pulpsters after thirty years, and at which I had met Kerry. The
reunion had led to murder and a case of plagiarism, among other
things . . . but that was another story.

"I thought you were going to have something to drink," Kerry said. "If you don't want a diet soda, I can make coffee."

"Not right now." My stomach was jumpy enough as it was, looking for something to digest, without putting caffein into it. "Aren't you going to ask me how my day was?"

"How was your day?"

"Lousy," I said.

"How come?"

"Well, to start it off, Eberhardt found us an office."

"Oh boy. Where?"

"On O'Farrell, near Van Ness."

I told her about it. She laughed when I mentioned the brass testicles on the light fixture, but by the time I finished, she was wearing a serious expression.

"It doesn't sound too bad, really," she said. "But are you sure . . . ?"

"No, I'm not sure. Let's not get into that again, okay?"

"Okay. When does the partnership open for business?"

"On Monday. Eb went out shopping for office furniture today. Mine's being delivered tomorrow afternoon."

"Well, all I can say is I hope it works out."

"Not as much as I hope so," I said. "Meanwhile, I picked up a three-day job this afternoon—my last solo investigation." I did not like the sound or taste of those last four words as I said them.

Kerry said, "Is it anything interesting?"

"Not particularly," and I told her about Haruko Gage and her secret admirer.

"Oh, I don't know," Kerry said, "it sounds kind of interesting to me."

"Yeah? Why?"

"It appeals to my romantic nature. You know, the mystery of it. It's a little frightening to have a determined secret admirer, but it's also pretty exciting."

"Mrs. Gage didn't seem to think so."

"Not that she let on. But then why did she wait so long to call in a detective?"

"She's a materialist. She likes expensive jewelry."

"I'll bet that's not all, though."

"Maybe not. Listen, how would you like to go visit a bath with me tonight?"

"What?"

"A public bath. You know, with other people."

"Are you being funny?"

"Nope. I thought I'd stop in and talk to one of Mrs. Gage's ex-boyfriends for a few minutes; it happens he works evenings in a Japanese bathhouse on Pine Street."

She made a face. Then her expression changed shape and became thoughtful. "A Japanese bathhouse?" she said. "I've never been inside one of those and I've always wondered what they're like."

"Likewise. So tonight we can both find out."

"All right. But I'm not going to *take* any public bath. I'd be too embarrassed."

"How about a private bath with me later on?"

"I don't think we'd both fit in the tub."

"There's always the shower."

"Mmm. We'll see."

Yeah, I thought, you bet we will.

She said, "But right now I'm hungry. I imagine you must be too."

"Starving."

"Well, we'd better go out somewhere. I don't have much here. What do you want to eat?"

"Do I get a choice?"

"Within reason."

"I want a New York steak about three inches thick," I said. "With sautéed mushrooms and a baked potato loaded down with sour cream and chives and bacon bits. And some sourdough French bread. And a pint or two of good ale."

"I'll just bet you do. And how *is* your diet going, anyway?"

"Peachy keen," I said.

"How much weight have you lost so far?"

"Two pounds."

"Is that all? You should have lost more than that. You haven't been cheating, have you?"

"No, I haven't been cheating. I've been grazing a lot, according to your mad dictates. And eating eggs—cartons of eggs. Cluck, cluck."

"That's good. I mean that you're not cheating. But you shouldn't eat too many eggs."

"What?"

"They're full of cholesterol."

"I thought you told me to eat eggs three times a day."

"I did not tell you that. I said they were high in protein and you should have them once or twice a day. Two meals and four eggs, maximum. With grapefruit to counteract the cholesterol."

"I hate grapefruit."

"Does that mean you haven't eaten any?"

"I didn't know I was supposed to."

"I *told* you. Don't you ever listen?"

"Not when somebody's trying to get me to eat grapefruit."

"Selective hearing," she said, "that's what you've got."

"Nuts," I said. "I don't care what you say, I'm going to have a steak tonight. Just the thought of one makes me weak."

"I never said you couldn't have a steak. It's the baked potato with all the trimmings and the sourdough bread and the two pints of ale you can't have."

"Then what do I get with the steak?"

"Black coffee and a green salad with lemon juice."

"Green salad with lemon juice. God."

"It's good for you. Where do you want to go?"

"I don't care," I said. "Just so long as we get there fast."

We ate at a place in one of the large downtown hotels that specialized in steaks. They sliced any cut of meat to order right in front of you, as soon as you came in, and I told the chef I wanted a sixteen-ounce New York done rare. Normally I like my steak medium rare, but tonight I was after red meat, the bloodier the better. It made me feel primitive as hell, like a caveman out on his first date.

When the steak arrived at our table I managed to eat it like a civilized human being, if just barely. I was even able to get down

most of the green salad with lemon juice. Kerry watched me with
a little awe in her expression. You'd have thought she had never seen
a starving man wolf food before.

After the waiter cleared away the remains we sat and talked for
a while over coffee. My stomach was full and I was happy. It doesn't
take much to make me happy—just a good meal, an attractive
woman, a pulp magazine to read, and a job to do. Maybe I *was* a
primitive, after all.

I let her pay the check for a change. She could afford it; she was
a highly paid copywriter for one of San Francisco's largest ad agencies and I was only a poorly paid private eye who was going to be
even more poorly paid once I had to start divvying with Eberhardt.
Then we went and got my car and I drove over to Pine and straight
out to Tamura's Baths. The sooner I got my little talk with Ken
Yamasaki over and done with, the sooner I could go have an Italian
shower with Kerry. Italian showers were much better than Japanese
baths. The kind I had in mind were, anyhow.

The building that housed the baths was nondescript enough—a
narrow brick structure, two stories high, flanked by an apartment
house and a corner grocery. I found a parking space two doors down
and we walked over to it through a drizzle that was more mist than
rain. A luminous clock in the window of the grocery said that the
time was 9:35.

At the door to the bathhouse, Kerry said, "Are you sure it's all
right for women to go in here?"

"You don't see any signs that say otherwise, do you?"

"No, I guess not."

The only sign of any sort was tacked up alongside the entrance.
It said TAMURA'S JAPANESE BATHS • HOURS 10 A.M.–10 P.M. DAILY.
I moved past it and opened the door and let Kerry precede me into
a narrow, gloomy hallway illuminated by a single Japanese lantern.
At the far end was a set of stairs leading upward.

It was quiet in there; I couldn't hear anything except silence when
I shut the door. The stairs took us into an anteroom that contained
some rattan chairs, two more lanterns, and a reception desk with
nobody behind it. To one side was a screened archway that probably
led back to the baths.

We waited fifteen or twenty seconds and nothing happened:

nobody came into the anteroom, nobody made any sounds anywhere else in the building. Finally I called, "Hello! Anybody here?" All that got me was an echo and more silence.

Kerry said, "Where is everybody?"

"Good question. The place can't be closed; it's not ten yet and the front door was unlocked."

"Maybe we should go look behind that screen."

"That must be where the baths are."

"So? Are you afraid I'll see something I've never seen before?"

"Fat chance of that."

She stuck her tongue out at me.

I went over and around the screen, with Kerry at my heels. Another corridor, this one lighted by more lanterns, with several doorways opening off it and another doorway at the far end. The first few doorways opened into dressing cubicles, all of them empty, a couple in which towels had been carelessly tossed on the floor; the ones beyond opened into the bathing areas. There were four of these —large rooms separated by movable, opaque screens, each room containing a waist-deep sunken tile tub large enough for half a dozen people, with bamboo mats on the floor around the rim. None of the rooms was occupied, although a few of the mats appeared to be wet.

"So this is what a Japanese bathhouse looks like," Kerry said. "It's a little disappointing. I expected something more exotic."

I didn't say anything. Something was wrong here; I could feel it in the air now, like little stirrings of bad wind. The place shouldn't have been empty, not with the front door unlocked. And if those towels on the floor and the wet mats were any indication, the people who had been here had left in a hurry. Not too long ago, either.

We were standing inside one of the bathing rooms. I said abruptly, "Stay here a minute, will you?"

"Why? What's the matter?"

"Just stay here. I'll be right back."

I left her before she could argue and went down to the end of the corridor. The door there was open about halfway; on the other side I could see part of a desk with a lamp burning on it and some filing cabinets. An office—Tamura's, maybe, if somebody named Tamura still ran the place. I put the tips of my fingers against the door and shoved it open all the way.

The first thing I saw was that the desk chair had been overturned. Then I saw the scattered shards of broken glass, and the spots of red on the wall. And then, when I took two steps inside and another two sideways, I saw the rest of the blood, on the floor and on the lower part of the wall, and the Japanese whose blood it had been.

He was lying crumpled against the baseboard; there wasn't any doubt that he was dead. The thing that had killed him was lying there too, bright-stained and gleaming in the light from the desk lamp.

He had been hacked to death with a samurai sword.

Five

My stomach turned over and the steak I'd eaten seemed to rise into the back of my throat in a bile-soaked lump. For a couple of seconds I thought I was going to throw it up. I looked away from the body, swallowed, and kept on swallowing until my throat unclogged.

Red meat, I thought, *the bloodier the better . . .*

I wanted to get out of there, but I had been a cop too many years and I had walked in on too many homicide scenes; instinct took me a few steps closer to the dead man, to where the scatter of glass shards and the spatters and ribbons of blood began. He'd been in his sixties, bald, lean, wearing a shirt and tie and a pair of herringbone slacks. I had never seen him before.

The broken glass came from a framed, blown-up photograph, about fifteen inches square, that had either fallen or been pulled down from the wall. It lay face up, so that when I bent forward I could see that it was a grainy black-and-white print of three Japanese men, all in their late teens or early twenties, standing in front of a wire-mesh fence with some buildings behind it in the distance. They had their arms around one another and they were smiling. One of them, the man in the middle, wore an oddly designed medallion looped around his neck; he might have been the dead man on the floor thirty or forty years ago, but as hacked and bloody as the corpse was, I couldn't be sure.

There was not much else to see in the office. Two closed doors,one in the side wall that was probably a closet, the other in the back wall that figured to be a rear exit. A few sheets of paper on the floor—what looked to be ledger pages with columns of numbers on them, dislodged from the desk. But there hadn't been much of a struggle; the killer had come in with the sword, or found it here in the office when he arrived, and struck more or less without warning.

The body kept drawing my eyes, magnetically. I started to back away from it. It was warm in there, too warm: the radiator along the side wall was turned up and burbling faintly. And the smell of death was making me light-headed. They tell you blood has no odor, but you can smell it just the same—a kind of brackish-sweet stench. It was heavy in the air now, along with the lingering foulness of evacuated bowels. Always those same odors at scenes like this one, where blood has been spilled and someone has died by violence. Always the same overpowering smell of death.

Footsteps sounded behind me in the corridor. "Hey, where are you?" Kerry's voice called. "What's going on?"

Christ. I swung around to fill the doorway and block her view. "Don't come in here."

She stopped moving and stared at me. She could see it in my face, the reflection of what I'd been looking at on the office floor; fright kindled in her eyes.

"There's a dead man in here," I said. "Murdered with a sword. It's pretty messy."

"My God! Who—?"

"I don't know."

"Not the man you came to see?"

"No. Much older. Probably the proprietor."

I got my handkerchief out, wrapped it around my hand, and then stepped into the corridor and pulled the door shut. I was afraid she might take it into her head to go have a look for herself. With Kerry, you never knew what she was liable to do.

She said, "Brr," and hugged herself the way you do when you feel a sudden chill. "That must be why nobody's here."

I nodded. And why everybody left in such a hurry, I thought. Ken Yamasaki and whoever else was in the baths must have heard the commotion, maybe even seen who did the killing. And instead of hanging around to call the police, they'd all run scared. But why *all* of them? Why Yamasaki? He was an employee; the police would have no trouble finding that out, and that he'd been here tonight. There was no sense in him running off with the rest of them.

Unless *he* was the murderer . . .

"Come on," I said, and took Kerry's hand and pulled her along into the reception area. I dipped my chin toward one of the rattan visitor's chairs. "Sit down over there—and try not to touch anything."

She did what I told her without saying anything. I moved over to the desk, used the handkerchief to lift the telephone receiver, and dialed the all-too-familiar number of the Hall of Justice.

The first prowl-car cops got there in ten minutes, and the Homicide boys showed up fifteen minutes after that. The inspector in charge was a guy named McFate, Leo McFate. We knew each other slightly, and were always civil in what little dealings we had—he'd been in General Works until Eberhardt's retirement got him transferred to the Homicide Detail—but I sensed that McFate didn't like me much. I had a pretty fair idea why, too, and it was none of the usual stuff that causes clashes between cops and private detectives; no jealousy or distrust or any of that. No, it had to do with the fact that McFate was a social climber. He went to the opera and the symphony and the ballet, and he got his name mentioned in the gossip columns from time to time, usually in connection with some local lady of means, and he dressed in tailored suits and hand-made ties and always looked like he was on his way to a wedding or a wake.

He didn't like me because he thought I was a coarse, sloppy, pulp-reading peon. Which I was, and the hell with Leo McFate.

He had nothing much to say when he and the others breezed in, except for a curt "Where is the deceased?" Deceased, yet. He didn't talk like a cop; he talked like Philo Vance. Or a political appointee in Sacramento, which was what he aspired to be someday, according to rumor. He had the demeanor for it, you couldn't deny that. Tall, muscled, imposing; what my grandmother would have called "a fine figure of a man." Dark brown hair going gray at the temples. A nifty brown mustache to go with a pair of nifty brown eyes. He even had a goddamn cleft in his chin like Robert Mitchum's.

I showed him where the deceased was. McFate spent a couple of minutes looking at the body and the bloody sword and the other stuff on the floor. I watched him do that from out in the hallway; I had no inclination to go in there again, and from where I was, the office desk blocked my view of the dead man. Then McFate had some words with the assistant coroner and with one of the members of the lab crew. Then he turned and came back out to where I was standing.

"What time did you find him?" he asked.

"About nine-forty. Three or four minutes before I called the Hall."

"When you got here, was the place this deserted?"

"Yes." I told him the way I figured that, and he nodded.

"How did you get in?"

"The front door was unlocked; we just walked in. We took a look around back here when we didn't find anybody at the reception desk."

"We?"

"Me and the lady out there. Kerry Wade."

"Am I to understand you came here to use the baths?" The words were innocent enough, but he managed to make them sound faintly supercilious, as if he were amused at the idea of rabble like me indulging in a Japanese bath.

I said, "No, we didn't come here to use the baths. We came here because I wanted to talk to one of the employees on a business matter."

"Which employee? Tamura?"

"Is Tamura the dead man?"

"Yes. Simon Tamura."

"How do you know that already?"

"Because we have a file on him. He was Yakuza."

"The hell he was," I said, surprised.

"The hell he wasn't."

"So that's it. A gang killing. No wonder everybody got out of here in a hurry, including the employees."

"Mmm," McFate said. "Which employee did you come here to see?"

"Ken Yamasaki."

McFate repeated the name. He wasn't writing down any of this conversation; he had a photographic memory and he was proud of the fact that he could quote verbatim interrogations that had lasted thirty minutes. I knew that about him because it had been in one of the gossip columns, back when I was still reading the newspapers. "What sort of business did you have with Yamasaki?" he asked.

"Nothing that involves the Yakuza," I said. "Or Tamura's death."

"Suppose you let me be the judge of that."

I was beginning to like him even less than he liked me. But the world is full of assholes, and you have to be tolerant if you want to keep the peace. So I told him in a nice, even, tolerant voice that Ken Yamasaki was an old boyfriend of Haruko Gage, who had hired me to find out the name of the secret admirer who was sending her presents in the mail.

It must have sounded silly to McFate; it even sounded a little silly to me, the way I explained it. He gave me a look that was half patronage and half watered-down pity. "The detective business must have fallen on hard times," he said, "if that's the kind of case you're taking on."

"You take what you can get these days," I said evenly.

"I understand Eberhardt is going into business with you," he said. "Soon, isn't it?"

"Next week."

"He would have been better off if he'd stayed on the force." McFate smiled as if to take the sting out of the words and then added, "If you don't mind my saying so."

I let it blow by. Assholes pass bad wind all the time; that was what you had to remember in dealing with them.

He said, "Do you know where Yamasaki lives?"

"No. He's not listed in the phone book."

"Did you know Simon Tamura when he was alive?"

"No. I never even heard of him before today."

"And you've had no recent case involving the Yakuza?"

"I've never had any case involving the Yakuza."

"So be it," McFate said. "Why don't you go sit with your lady friend for the time being. I may have more questions a little later."

"Sure. As long as we can get out of here before midnight."

I left him and went back into the reception area and plunked myself down in the rattan chair next to Kerry. She said, "What's the matter? Why are you scowling?"

"Something McFate just told me," I said. "The dead man back there was Yakuza."

"What's Yakuza?"

"Japanese gangster outfit. Sort of like the Mafia."

"Oh God," she said.

"Take it easy. It's not as ominous as it sounds."

"No?"

"No. I don't know much about them, but they're big in Japan and East Asia and they're starting to get a foothold over here. Prostitution, extortion, that sort of thing. But they only prey on other Japanese—merchants and tourists, mostly."

"Oh. Then the dead man . . . do you know his name yet?"

"Simon Tamura. He ran this place, I imagine."

"Then he was killed by other Yakuza? One of those underworld execution things?"

"Looks that way," I said. "The Yakuza are supposed to believe that they're descendants of samurai warriors. And Tamura was murdered with a samurai sword. A ritual killing, maybe, to avenge some breaking of the Yakuza code."

"Well, thank God you're not mixed up in it, for a change. It's bad enough that you had to find the body. And that I had to be here with you."

"No argument about that."

"One murder case after another ever since I've known you," she said. "One of these days . . ."

"One of these days what?"

"You know what I was going to say."

"Yeah. But I've lived this long; I intend to go on living a good while longer."

"I hope so. Sometimes . . . damn it, sometimes you scare hell out of me."

"Sometimes, babe," I said, "I scare hell out of myself."

We lapsed into silence, but it was all right between us because Kerry reached over after a few seconds and took hold of my hand. Her fingers were dry and chill—unlike the room itself, which was as warm as Tamura's office. It started me sweating, and I stood up finally and fumbled with the knob on the radiator until I got the heat shut down.

Cops went in and out, and what seemed like a long time later two white-outfitted interns clumped in with a body bag. Almost immediately after they disappeared toward the office, McFate reappeared and headed toward Kerry and me. We both got on our feet.

"Tamura was definitely Yakuza," McFate said without preamble. "He had one of their tattoos on his chest—a samurai warrior battling a dragon. And his desk is full of incriminating evidence. He was a local *mizu shobai* kingpin."

I had no idea what that last meant, but I was not going to give him the satisfaction of admitting it. I figured he'd tell us anyway, and he did.

"*Mizu shobai* means 'water business,' " he said in his supercilious way. "Extortion from Japanese bars, restaurants, and night clubs in the Bay Area—a variation on the old protection racket. Very lucrative."

"Which means he probably had rivals."

"Probably. We'll find out." He paused. "Do you still plan to talk to Ken Yamasaki?"

"That depends," I said, "on whether or not he had anything to do with Tamura's death."

"Then you had better not try to contact him until you find out."

"I won't."

"Good. You don't intend to do any investigating into Yakuza activities, do you?"

"No. Why should I?"

"You shouldn't, if what you told me earlier is true."

"It's true. I don't lie to the police, McFate."

"But you do go off on tangents now and then."

"Meaning what?"

"Meaning you lost your license once," McFate said, "and it would be a shame if it happened again. So I'd advise you to confine your present activities to tracking down secret admirers. Leave the Yakuza to us."

I could feel myself getting hot; he was rubbing salt into old wounds now. But making an issue of it with him was not going to buy me anything except trouble. I made myself say, "You don't have

to worry about me," in a neutral voice. "Is it all right if we go now?"
"You can go, but I want to ask Ms. Wade a few questions before
she leaves. For the sake of corroboration."

Kerry looked at me. I said, "I can use some fresh air. I'll wait for
you in the car."

She nodded, and McFate gave her one of his charming smiles, and
I beat it out of there before I did or said something stupid. There
were a couple of reporter types hanging around out front, but they
didn't seem to know who I was; I glared at them the way cops do
and they didn't bother me. I walked up to the end of the block,
letting the wind and the steady drizzle cool me off. When I came
back to the car I sat behind the wheel, with the window rolled down
a little, and watched the clock in the grocery store window.

Five more minutes passed before Kerry came out. She said as she
slid in beside me, "Whew, am I glad to get out of there!"

"Did McFate give you a hard time?"

"Not really. But the way he kept looking at me, I was afraid he
might try to make a pass. What's the matter with him, anyway?"

"He's an asshole," I said, and let it go at that.

We didn't take a shower together that night. We didn't do
anything together that night, primitive or otherwise. The combina-
tion of the murder and McFate had knocked out all of my amorous
feelings and intentions, and Kerry wasn't much interested either. So
we said good night in the car in front of her building, and I drove
home and crawled into bed alone.

Some day, all right. A real prizewinner.

Six

I was up at eight-thirty in the morning, and showered and shaved
and in the kitchen for breakfast before nine. The thought of eggs
in any form, particularly accompanied by grapefruit, started an un-
pleasant burbling in my stomach. So I hunted around in the refriger-

ator for something else nonfattening to eat, but all I could come up with were celery stalks and carrots and some yogurt that Kerry had bought for me. Pineapple yogurt, the container said, fruit on the bottom. Yeah, I thought, but not on the bottom of my stomach. I put it back into the fridge, along with the celery stalks and the carrots, and opened a can of V-8 juice. I could get some solid food into me later on.

The telephone rang while I was pouring coffee. I went into the bedroom and hauled up the receiver, and Eberhardt said, "Find any more bodies this morning? Or is the day still too young?"

"Not funny," I said. "You heard about last night, huh?"

"Me and a few million others. You ought to start reading the papers regularly; you get mentioned in them enough these days."

"That's one of the reasons I don't read them. Front-page stuff this time?"

"Sure. A guy gets hacked up with a samurai sword—that's good copy. In particular when he's a big noise in the local branch of the Yakuza."

"How many times did my name get taken in vain?"

"Only once. Not much ink at all. Just that you and Kerry found the body."

"Kerry got mentioned, too? Damn McFate. I thought he might at least leave her out of it."

"Leo likes to see his name in the papers," Eberhardt said. "He figures everybody else does too."

"Listen, Eb, I'm not mixed up in Simon Tamura's murder. Or with the Yakuza. I went to those baths to talk to one of the employees—not Tamura, another guy—on a minor domestic case."

"Did I ask?"

"I just wanted you to know."

"Well, I thought it was something like that. I figured you'd have told me if you were messing with anything as big-league as the Yakuza. Besides, you're not dumb enough to take Kerry into a place that fronts for a gang of thugs."

"Thanks—I think."

"Don't mention it. You going to be busy today?"

"Some. Why?"

"I bought a desk and a chair and a couple of other things yesterday," he said. "They're being delivered this afternoon. I thought maybe you'd want to help me move things around."

"What time is the delivery?"

"Sometime after two."

"Well, that ought to work out okay. My stuff's coming out of storage and over to the office around that time. I should be able to get there by then."

"Good," he said. "Looking forward to it, paisan."

That makes one of us, I thought.

I dialed Kerry's number, to find out if she'd read the newspaper thing too, but there was no answer. She'd already left for Bates and Carpenter, the ad agency where she worked.

So I took the directory out of the nightstand drawer, looked up the number of the registrar's office at City College and then punched it out. The woman who answered said that Nelson Mixer was still out sick. I found Mixer's home number, and when I called it a man's voice came on after five rings. He sounded a little miffed, as if I had interrupted him at something. Sleeping, maybe, or taking medicine; his voice was hoarse. I asked him if he was Nelson Mixer and he said he was and I said, "I wonder if you'd be interested in purchasing some aluminum siding at a premium price—" and he hung up on me. I grinned as I cradled the receiver. Now I knew where to find him this morning.

I drank my coffee in the kitchen, trying not to listen to the empty noises my stomach was making. Then I spent ten minutes doing the exercises the muscle therapist had given me to strengthen the damaged motor nerve in my left arm and shoulder. The same gunman who had put Eberhardt in a coma for seventeen days back in August had pumped a bullet into me, too. I had had a lot of stiffness in the arm for a while, and I still had some off and on, particularly after any kind of physical activity. But it wasn't so bad any more, as a result of time and the muscle therapy. Most days I had no pain or stiffness at all and I was reminded of the trouble only when I tried, without thinking, to use the arm for something. I still had a three- or four-percent impairment, according to the therapist. The goal was one percent, which was as close to normal as the old wing was going to get.

My watch said it was just nine-thirty when I shrugged into my

overcoat and put on my hat and left the flat. I hoped Nelson Mixer
had something useful to tell me. As things stood, with Ken Yamasaki
unavailable to me for the time being, the only other name on my
list was Edgar Ogada. And I wanted very much to find out the
identify of Haruko Gage's secret admirer. Not because it was any big
deal; it wasn't. Just because I wanted my last solo investigation, my
last little fling, to be a successful one.

Nelson Mixer's residence turned out to be a small house on 46th
Avenue, just off Balboa and not far from either Sutro Heights Park
or the ocean. It was one of the stucco rowhouses that a builder
named Dolger had strung out over the avenues in the 1930s—the
kind Malvina Reynolds had referred to as "ticky-tacky houses" in her
sixties protest song, "Little Boxes." Each one attached to its neighbors, like links in a giant chain, with a little patch of ground in front
and a garage under the living room windows. When the garage was
open it would look like a gaping mouth under a couple of bulging
rectangular eyes.

Two things set Mixer's house off from those of his neighbors. One
was the fact that it was painted a bilious urine-yellow color uncompli-
mented by bright green trim. The other was the Christmas tree
prominently displayed in one of the front windows: pink-flocked,
decorated with silver tinsel and sparkly blue ornaments. If there had
been a city ordinance against visual pollution—and there ought to
have been—they could have slapped Mixer with a hell of a fine.

The curb in front was empty; I put my car there and stepped out
into the same kind of light, steady drizzle we had had last night.
December in San Francisco usually brings decent weather, but not
this year. It had been raining off and on for three weeks now and
I was pretty sick of it. I was starting to feel like an overwatered
houseplant: much more of this and I would start to rot.

I ran up the yellow stucco staircase to one of those burglar-proof
wrought iron gates that protected the front stoop. It kept me standing out in the rain while I pushed the doorbell and waited for
somebody to respond. I waited a good minute before that happened;
then the door clicked open and eased inward and a face peered at
me around the edge. It was a white face, sort of vulpine, topped with
a wild shock of red hair that clashed painfully with the yellow walls

and green trim. It peered at me being rained on outside the gate,
blinked a couple of times, and poked out a little farther from behind
the door on a long scrawny neck.

"Yes?" the face said warily. "What do you want?"

"Are you Nelson Mixer?"

"I am. Who are you?"

I told him who I was and what I did for a living. His eyes got wide
and popped a little, as if I'd told him I was Benito Mussolini come
back from the dead; the white skin turned even whiter. He yanked
the door open all the way, more a reflex action than anything else,
and I was looking at the rest of him. There wasn't much to see,
really. He was about five-six and weighed in at a strapping one-
twenty, all of which was encased in a royal blue bathrobe with
gold-leaf dragons emblazoned on it. He could have been thirty-five
or he could have been forty-five. He could also have been slightly
screwball, if the way he was gawping at me was any indication.

"Private detective?" he said. "My God! What do you want? Who
sent you?"

"Nobody sent me, Mr. Mixer. I—"

"Clara's father? Is he the one?"

"I'm afraid I don't know anyone named—"

"Well, you tell him I never touched her. You hear me? It's all a
pack of lies. All I did was tutor her."

"Pardon me?"

"Tutor, tutor. You know what tutor means, don't you?"

"Of course I know what—"

"There was never anything between Clara and me. No physical
contact of any kind. I don't even find her attractive; I've never liked
women with big behinds. Tell him *that*, the old fool."

"Look, Mr. Mixer . . . "

"Nellie!" a woman's voice called from somewhere inside the
house. "Nellie, what are you doing out there?"

"Oh my God," Mixer said. He glanced over his shoulder, looked
back at me again. Sudden guilt had spread like jam over his vulpine
features.

"*Nell*ie?"

He half-turned. "Stop that yelling!" he yelled. "I'll be there in a
minute, Darlene."

"It's pretty wet out here," I said when his attention returned to me. "How about buzzing me in so we can talk?"

"Hah," he said. "I don't care if you *drown* out there."

"You're all heart. Who's Darlene?"

"What?"

"Your friend inside. Darlene."

"She's not my friend," he said quickly. "She's one of my students."

"I called up City College a while ago," I said. "They told me you were too sick to teach today."

"Too sick to leave the *house*. Yes, that's right. I was just, ah, tutoring Darlene."

"In your bathrobe?"

He looked down at himself as if he'd forgotten he was wearing the robe. Little red splotches appeared on his cheeks; they matched the color of his hair. "I, ah . . . that is, I . . . coffee, I spilled coffee on myself while we were . . ." He quit sputtering all of a sudden, drew himself up, bared his teeth in a foxy snarl, and said, "I don't have to explain anything to you. Go away. Go tell Clara's father I'll sue him if he doesn't stop harassing me."

"I'm *not* working for Clara's father," I said, getting it out fast because he had started to shut the door. "I don't know anybody named Clara. I'm here about Haruko Gage."

The door stayed open about halfway. "Who?"

"Haruko Gage. She's been—"

"Who the hell is Haruko Gage?"

"You don't remember her, is that it?"

"Nellie!"

"No," Mixer said, "I don't remember her. Who is she?"

"A former student of yours. You asked her to move in with you about three years ago."

"I did what?"

"Or don't you remember that either?"

"Nellie!"

"Haruko Gage? Good God," he said, "not Haruko Fujita? The little Japanese girl who was studying art?"

"Probably; Gage is her married name. Or do you routinely ask Japanese girls to live with you?"

That got me another foxy snarl. "You can't talk to me like that. I won't allow it."

"You can't let me stand out here in the rain, but you're doing it anyway. Haruko Gage has been receiving anonymous presents in the mail—expensive jewelry, one with a love note. You wouldn't know anything about that, would you?"

"Nel-lie!"

"Goddamn it," Mixer said. "Be quiet, Darlene!"

"Well, hurry up, can't you?" the woman's voice called. She sounded young. "I'm getting cold sitting around here like this. Besides, I can't get your stupid movie camera to work right."

The red flush came back into Mixer's face, dragging the guilt along with it. He said something that sounded like "Gah," jerked his head back, and slammed the door.

I shoved my finger against the doorbell button, kept it there. At the end of thirty or forty seconds the door opened and Mixer said, "Go away, leave me alone! I'll call the police!" And the door banged shut again.

I gave it up. I went back down the stairs and got into the car and used my handkerchief for a rain towel. Now I knew what Alice felt like after she'd spent some time in Wonderland; it was as if I had just done verbal battle with the Mad Hatter. Or, more appropriately, it seemed, the Mad Lecher.

Cross Mixer off the list? What with Clara and Darlene and Christ knew how many others eager for his tutoring, it didn't seem likely that he would be writing anonymous love notes and blowing a wad of money on fancy jewelry for Haruko Gage. Still, he was a screwball; and you never know what a screwball might do. I wanted at least one more session with Mixer, under different and more conventional circumstances, before I wrote him off.

The thing about him that bothered me most was his ability to attract Haruko and Clara and Darlene and presumably a whole dewy-eyed and horny legion of college-age females. What the hell did any of them see in a scrawny, color-blind, unlovely specimen like him? Why would women even *consider* dropping their drawers for the Nelson Mixers of the world?

It was nagging little questions like this that made you wonder about life's fundamental equity.

*   *   *   *

Somebody was tailing me.

I spotted the car six blocks from Mixer's house, when it followed me into a turn east on Geary Boulevard. White Ford about two years old, with one of those whip antennas that CB subscribers have on their vehicles. Two people in it, but that was all I could tell; they hung back pretty good and stayed in another lane and the rain made it difficult to see clearly through the rear window. I couldn't make out the license plate either.

Well, I was getting old. In my salad days, even though these guys appeared to be doing all the things you're supposed to do to conduct a successful shadow job, I would have tumbled to them within five minutes of leaving Pacific Heights. My flat was where they'd picked me up, of course; I remembered seeing the Ford as I headed down Laguna to Geary. They'd hung around on 46th Avenue waiting for me to get done with Mixer, and now here they were again.

But hell, the last thing I'd have expected today was a tail. The idea of it annoyed me—and made me a little uneasy. Who were they? What did they think they were going to find out by shagging me around the city?

I swung over into the far left lane and made a left turn on 30th Avenue; drove past Presidio Middle School and turned right on Clement and went down to 25th Avenue and turned left again. The white Ford stayed with me all the way, still hanging back far enough so that I couldn't get a look at the occupants or read the license plate. No doubt at all now that the Ford was there to keep me company.

I drove straight down 25th at a nice easy pace and passed between the stone pillars that marked the entrance to Seacliff, one of San Francisco's ritzier residential districts. Left on Scenic Way and left again on Seacliff Avenue, past a lot of elegant homes strung out along the cliffside and commanding panoramic views of the Golden Gate. The street forked after a few blocks, with the main branch blending into El Camino del Mar and leading up to Land's End; Seacliff Avenue hooked to the right and dead-ended after about a block and a half. I stayed on Seacliff. The Ford was two blocks behind me as I veered that way.

On my left were more houses and on my right was a parking area bounded by a long cyclone fence. Beyond the fence, a steep slope fell away to China Beach—a narrow inlet that had been a campsite for Chinese fishermen last century and now was a locally popular sunbathing spot. Nobody was down there today, in the rain and with the surf crashing heavy and white over the offshore rocks; the beach was all but invisible under the high tide. And the parking area was empty.

I cut into the lot, made a fast U-turn, and slid out onto the street pointing the way I'd come. I had timed it right: the Ford had already veered in and slowed to a crawl, and there was no place for them to go. I got the license number and I got a good look at their faces as I drove by—making it obvious so they'd be sure to know I was on to them. Two men, big and tough-looking, the driver wearing a mustache and a startled look, the passenger with a nose like a blob of brownish putty.

Both of them were Japanese.

I kept on going past them, turned right on El Camino del Mar, went up the hill to the Palace of the Legion of Honor, and drove past it and through the Lincoln Park Golf Course—a loop that took me back to Geary. There was no sign of the white Ford. Either they'd given it up on their own or they'd used the CB and whoever they'd called had told them to lay off. But this wasn't going to be the end of it. I had a bad feeling that they would be back pretty soon, and maybe not just to follow me around.

One word kept running around inside my head. It scared me some and made me nervous and puzzled the hell out of me because I had no idea of the *why* of it.

The word was Yakuza.

Seven

I stopped at a service station on Geary and 25th Avenue and called Harry Fletcher, my contact at the local office of the Department of Motor Vehicles. I relayed the license number of the white Ford and asked him to run it through the computer and find out who the car was registered to. He said he'd do that as soon as he could, give him half an hour.

I glanced at my watch as I hung up: a couple of minutes after eleven. Too early to head down to South San Francisco for a talk with Edgar Ogada; his father had told me Edgar wouldn't be around until after noon sometime. Too early for lunch, too, but to hell with standing on ceremony. My stomach was yammering for something its juices could go to work on. Funny thing about tension: sometimes it robs you of your appetite and sometimes it makes you ravenously hungry. The damned diet had tipped the scales to ravenous this time, Yakuza or no Yakuza.

There were some good restaurants on outer Clement, only a few blocks away, so I drove over there and found a café I'd eaten in before. They had several things on the menu that looked inviting— steak sandwich, Reuben sandwich, bacon cheeseburger—but I girded myself and ordered cottage cheese and fruit with RyKrisp. I would have had the diet plate, which included a ground sirloin patty, but that made me think of red meat and the way Simon Tamura's bloody corpse had looked there on the floor of his office. I wanted nothing to do with red meat for a while. I'd had enough bad dreams last night as it was.

The cottage cheese and fruit weren't bad, considering; at least they eased the hunger pangs. While I ate I tried to come up with an answer to why the Yakuza would have had me followed. Because I was the one who'd found Tamura's body? Well, maybe. That, plus the fact that I was a private investigator, might have made them wonder what I'd been doing at the bathhouse; that part of it hadn't been in the papers, evidently. But I had figured the killing for a vendetta job and so had McFate. If it was, why would the Yakuza be sniffing around me? And if it wasn't, why not just brace me somewhere and ask me if I knew anything? Why the tail instead?

All very mysterious and unsettling. And it got even more so when I used the café's public phone to ring back Harry Fletcher at the DMV.

The white Ford was registered to Kenneth Yamasaki, 2610 California Street, San Francisco.

There was plenty of activity at the Ogada Nursery when I got there just past noon. Half a dozen vans and two pick-up trucks, some with the names of prominent florists painted on their sides, were pulled up on the blacktopped area fronting the greenhouses; and a mix of Caucasian and Oriental men were loading and unloading potted plants and flowers, clay pots, sacks of loam and mulch and fertilizer. They all seemed to be in a hurry, either because it was the lunch hour or because of the weather. The rain had stopped for the moment, but the dark threatening clouds to the west said it would begin again before long.

I parked out of the way and wandered over to one of the workers and asked him if Edgar Ogada was around. He told me to go look in the greenhouse, and pointed to the first building in the nearest row.

It was cold and damp inside the big, high-roofed enclosure, and smelled thickly and richly of moist earth and growing things. Ferns and other house plants filled it—rows upon rows of them, in beds and in pots on long benches or hanging from a latticework of wire strung horizontally some eight feet off the ground. The only person in evidence was Ogada Senior; he was back toward the rear, doing something with one of the valves that operated a sprinkler system.

He looked at me without recognition when I reached him and said, "Afternoon, Mr. Ogada." He appeared even more tired than he had yesterday; his eyes had the dull sheen of someone who has been burning a lot of midnight oil. "I was here yesterday afternoon to speak with your son."

"Hai," he said, and nodded. "Yes, I remember."

"Would Edgar be here now?"

Another nod. "In the next shed . . . So. Here he comes."

I half-turned to follow the direction of his gaze. A young guy had just come through a door in the opaque fiberglass wall that adjoined the next greenhouse. As he approached I saw that he was about thirty, tallish, wiry, good-looking in a careless sort of way. Bristly mustache, hair that fanned down over his shoulders, eyes that had the light of mischief in them. He wore running shoes and faded Levi's and a sweatshirt with the sleeves cut off; on the front of the sweatshirt were the words NO NUKES in bright red letters.

"Hey, Pop," he said, "what happened to those live seafoam and shooting-star miniatures? I don't see them anywhere." Pop, like

Number One Son addressing Charlie Chan. He didn't even glance at me.

"Gone," his father said.

"Gone? You mean you sold them?"

"Yes."

"Pop, I told you yesterday morning the Crawley brothers wanted them. What's the matter? You going senile on me?"

Mr. Ogada didn't say anything. So I said, "Everybody forgets things now and then, particularly when they've been working hard."

The young guy, Edgar, put his eyes on me for the first time. There was no hostility in the look, nor even any annoyance; it was just a look with a question: Who are you?

I said, "I'd like to talk to you for a few minutes, if you don't mind. A personal matter."

"The washers in this valve need to be changed," Mr. Ogada said, "Will you do it, Edgar? I have invoices to prepare."

"If I've got time."

"*Hai,*" Mr. Ogada said, and bowed slightly in my direction, and went away toward the outside door.

Edgar said, "What's this personal matter you want to talk about?"

"A former girlfriend of yours. Haruko Gage."

His forehead wrinkled slightly; that was the extent of his reaction to Haruko's name. "Why?" he said. "Who are you, anyway?"

"A private detective." I gave him my name and showed him the photostat of my license. "Mrs. Gage hired me to investigate a little problem she's having."

"You mean Haruko's in trouble?"

"No, nothing like that."

I told him what the problem was, and he didn't react much to that either. A little surprise and a little puzzlement, nothing else.

"I don't get it," he said. "Anybody who'd do something like that has to be nuts."

"That's what Haruko is afraid of."

"But why talk to me? I don't know anything about it." He paused and frowned again. "Hey, she doesn't think *I'm* the one who's doing it, does she?"

"No. Your name was one of several she gave me—old boyfriends, men who've been serious about her in the past."

"Well, that lets me out. I've never been serious over any girl.
There's too many of 'em, you know? Too many *sakana* in the *umi.*"

"Uh-huh."

"We had some fun, Haruko and me," Edgar said. He grinned. "I
brought her here once and we were, you know, getting it on over at
the house and Pop almost caught us. *That* would have been a heavy
scene. Pop's old-fashioned; he doesn't think people ought to screw
unless they're married."

"Is that how your mother feels too?"

The grin vanished. "My mother's dead," he said in a different,
softer voice. "She died last summer. It's been rough on Pop; that's
why he works so hard."

Rough on Edgar, too, judging from his tone. I said, "How do you
feel about Haruko now that she's married?"

"Same as I've always felt about her. We're still friends, only
without the sex."

"No regrets about that?"

"A few, sure. I wouldn't mind getting it on with her again if she
ever dumps Art the Fart; we were good together, real good. But it's
no big deal. A guy can always get laid."

"I take it you don't like her husband much."

"He's a jerkoff. I don't know why she married him, unless it's
because he lets her tell him what to do. Or maybe he's Clark Kent
with his clothes on and Superman in the sack." He shrugged. "Who
knows why women do anything? I never could figure 'em out."

That makes two of us, brother, I thought. "Do you know Ken
Yamasaki?"

"Sure. Not too well, though. He thinks he's an intellectual; I don't
think I am."

"Could he be Haruko's secret admirer, do you think?"

"It wouldn't surprise me."

"How about Kinji Shimata?"

"Shimata . . . no, never heard of him."

"Nelson Mixer?"

"Is that somebody's name?"

"Yes. A history teacher at City College."

"I didn't go to college," he said and shrugged again.

I thanked him for his time, and he said, "Sure, I hope you find the nut," and I left him and went out of the greenhouse. Most of the vehicles and workers had disappeared; so had Ogada Senior. The black-veined clouds were overhead now, scudding along in front of the sharp west wind like bales of gangrenous wool.

The rain started again, hard driving bullets of it, before I was halfway to my car.

With the exception of Ken Yamasaki, I had exhausted the list of names Haruko Gage had given me and I hadn't learned much of anything so far. I had Yamasaki's address, but I couldn't look him up until I cleared it with Leo McFate. After having had my license suspended for a time five months ago, even though I hadn't done much of anything wrong to deserve it, I could not afford to get the cops miffed at me again. And I couldn't go down to the Hall to see McFate until four o'clock; he'd answered the homicide squeal last night, which meant he was working the four-to-midnight swing this week.

Another talk with Haruko seemed to be the only tack I had left. I could find out if she knew about Ken Yamasaki's apparent Yakuza connections, and I could ask her some more questions about her past, maybe get a few more names worth checking out.

I came back into San Francisco on the 19th Avenue exit off Highway 280, drove straight to Japantown, and managed to find the same parking spot near the Gage Victorian that I'd occupied yesterday. When I went up and rang the bell, Haruko herself opened the door. She was wearing a tight white sweater today, and a pair of form-fitting designer slacks, and her glossy black hair was piled high on her head and held in place by a lacquered Oriental comb. Artie must have licked his chops when he saw her dressed up like that. Even I had to admit that she looked pretty sexy.

"Oh, good," she said when she saw me. "Did you get my message?"

"Message?"

"The one I left on your answering machine."

"No, I didn't get it. I haven't been home."

"Are you here because you found out something. . . ?"

"I'm afraid not. I talked to Shimata and Mixer and Ogada, but no luck so far. I just wanted to ask you a few more questions."

"Damn," she said angrily, but the anger wasn't directed at me. "Well, I called you this morning because I received another package."

"Oh? The same sort as before?"

"Not exactly. Come in and I'll show you."

She led me into the cluttered, ersatz-antique parlor where we'd held yesterday's conference. On the coffee table were a small white gift box with the lid on and some package wrapping and twine. There was no sign of her wimpy husband.

I picked up the wrapping paper. All that was printed on it this time, in the familiar crabbed, childlike scrawl, was a single word: *Chiyoko.*

Haruko said, "He didn't mail it this time; he must have brought it here himself and left it on the porch beside the mailbox. Art found it at nine-thirty, when he went out to buy coffee."

"What does 'Chiyoko' mean?"

"It doesn't mean anything. It's my middle name." She seemed to think that needed explanation; she said, "If Japanese-Americans have middle names at all, they're usually American names; but my father liked to be different. Haruko Chiyoko. It sounds strange."

It didn't sound strange to me, but what did I know? I said, "So do you make a secret of it, then? Or is it common knowledge?"

She shrugged. "Everybody who knows me knows it's my middle name," she said. "I'm not ashamed of it."

"Is there anyone who calls you by that name?"

"No. No one ever has." She watched me put the wrapping paper back on the table and pick up the gift box. Then she said, "Whoever he is, he's getting bolder, isn't he."

"Not necessarily."

"It sure seems that way." Her expression turned wry. "And now he's not even sending me anything worthwhile."

"Pardon?"

"His latest present—it's not valuable like the others."

"Another piece of jewelry?"

"A medallion," she said in insulted tones. "An old, cheap, used one." She reached over and pulled the lid off the box I held in my hands. "There, you see? Damascene, that's all. It's probably not worth more than twenty dollars."

I stared at it. A lacquered thing shaped like a St. Christopher's medal, with an inlaid design comprised of gold and silver lines. Once it must have had a rich, high polish; now it was dulled and one corner was chipped. Through an eyehook on top was a loop of stiff, new rawhide, so that the medallion could be worn around the neck.

I kept on staring at it. Because I had seen it before—it, or one very similar. And I did not like the connection it formed in my mind; I didn't like it at all.

The medallion was what the young Simon Tamura had been wearing in the broken-framed photograph lying next to his corpse.

Eight

Haruko said, "What's the matter? Why are you looking at it that way?"

"Have you ever seen a medallion like this before?"

"I don't think so. Why?"

"So it's not a common type or design."

"No. It's just a piece of damascene."

"What's damascene?"

She told me: a process that involved chiseling fine lines on a steel foundation, inlaying them with gold and silver, corroding the steel with acid, and then lacquering and polishing. "They make damascene in Kyoto," she said. "One of the old arts."

"And it isn't expensive, even with the gold and silver inlays?"

"No. Not unless it's a large piece, where a lot of precious metal is used. You can buy most damascene for a few dollars."

I set the box down on the table again. "What about the design on the medallion?" I asked her. "Does that have any significance?"

"To me? No."

"Historical or religious significance, maybe?"

"Not that I know of. But I'm a Sansei; I was born here, not in Japan."

"Did you know Simon Tamura?"

The abrupt shift in questions made her blink. "The man who owns Tamura's Baths?"

"Yes."

"I met him when I was seeing Ken Yamasaki, and I saw him again a few months ago. Why are you asking about Mr. Tamura?"

"You didn't know he was murdered last night?"

"Murdered? My God, no."

"It was all over this morning's paper."

"We don't take the morning paper." She was frowning and she looked a little edgy now. "What happened to him?"

"Somebody hacked him to death with a samurai sword," I said. "In his office at the bathhouse. I had the bad luck to find the body when I went there to talk to your friend Yamasaki."

Her gaze slid away from my face and down to my hands, as if she were looking for bloodstains. A little shiver ran through her; you could see that violence, even the discussion of it, upset her. "I don't understand," she said after a time. "What does that have to do with me?"

"Maybe nothing. But there was a framed photograph beside Tamura's body that had been knocked off the wall—three young men, one of them Tamura, taken between thirty and forty years ago. He was wearing a medallion in the photo just like this one."

She started to speak, but there were thumping noises on the hall stairs just then and her mouth hinged shut on whatever the words were. Art Gage's voice called, "Haruko? Where are you?" and I heard him do some more thumping in the hall. But I kept my eyes on Haruko. Her face was pale; anxiety crouched like shadows behind the dull light in her eyes.

Gage came into the room with a big sheet of draftsman's paper flapping in one hand. He saw me, stopped, and said, "Oh." Then Haruko's expression registered on him and his reaction was almost Chaplinesque: a seriocomic look of shock and consternation, followed by a rush to her side and some solicitous pawing. She didn't look at him or try to move away. All she did was start gnawing on her lower lip like a beaver working on a twig.

"What is it, hon?" Gage asked her. When she didn't answer he swung his head and glared at me. "What did you say to her? Why is she—?"

"Your wife and I are having a private discussion, Mr. Gage," I said. "How about if you leave us alone so we can finish it."

He shook the sheet of draftsman's paper at me. It had some kind of fleur-de-lis design on it, intermingled with stylistic sunbursts, so the gesture was more humorous than threatening. Chaplin would have liked that too.

"Listen," he said, "I don't have to—"

"Art." She said it soft, with none of yesterday's sharpness, but he was so used to hearing it that it had the same effect: he shut his mouth immediately. "Go back to the studio," she said. "Go finish the design."

"But—"

"I'll tell you what this is about later."

He hesitated. "Well, if you're sure . . ."

"Go on, Artie."

He went. He was one of those people who were destined to wander through life delivering half-finished sentences, one of those people nobody ever listened to, and I felt a little sorry for him. But not much.

When I heard him on the stairs again I said to Haruko, "The times you saw Tamura—was he wearing anything that might have been this medallion? Take your time. Think about it."

She took fifteen or twenty seconds, with her eyes half shut. "I'm not sure," she said finally. "I think . . . I seem to remember a leather thong like that being around his neck. But I never saw what was on it."

"Suppose it was the medallion," I said. "Do you have any idea why anyone would want to send it to you?"

"No. God, no."

"Ken Yamasaki, maybe. Would he have a reason?"

She shook her head.

"Just how well do you know Yamasaki?"

"Not very well," she said. "I told you that yesterday. We dated off and on for a few weeks, that's all."

"What does he look like?"

The question puzzled her, but she answered it without questions of her own. "He's a year or two older than me, slim, sensitive-looking. He wears glasses."

So neither of the two guys in the white Ford this morning had been Yamasaki, even though the car was registered in Yamasaki's name. Curiouser and curiouser.

Haruko said, "You don't think that Ken . . . ?"

"I don't think anything, Mrs. Gage," I said. "I'm only trying to make some sense out of what's going on. What broke things up between you and Yamasaki?"

"I don't remember. Nothing specific; we just weren't compatible and we drifted apart."

"Did you know he and Simon Tamura were Yakuza?"

The word Yakuza had the effect of a small, sharp slap; she put a hand up to her face as if to rub away the sting. "Ken?" she said. "No, you must be wrong . . ."

"I don't think so. It's a certainty Tamura was one of them; take a look at today's paper. Yamasaki worked for him, and he disappeared from the baths last night after Tamura was killed. This morning a couple of hard-looking guys followed me around for a while in Yamasaki's car. I don't know how that looks to you, but to me it means he's connected."

She wagged her head again, loosely this time, as if what I'd just told her was too much to absorb all at once. She backed away from me, bumped into the coffee table, made a kind of graceless sidestep around it, and flopped onto the claw-footed couch. I watched her sit there, waiting for her to say something. All I heard was the thin whispering rhythm of the rain outside.

After awhile I went over and sat on the other end of the couch. "I'm sorry if I upset you, Mrs. Gage," I said. "But that's the way things are. I don't like them any more than you do."

She nodded. "It's just that . . . all of this about murder and the Yakuza . . ."

"I know, it scares me a little too."

"I thought detectives didn't get scared."

"Some don't, but I wouldn't want to be one of them. Fearless people aren't too bright, usually; they go banging around on their own little ego trips and wind up causing other people grief."

For some reason that seemed to reassure her. She nodded again, and pretty soon she said, "If Ken is or was Yakuza he never said anything about it to me. And I never heard it from anyone else."

"What about Tamura?"

"The same. I had no idea he was one of them."

"The last time you saw Yamasaki . . . how long ago was it?"

"A few months. Late this past summer."

"Before you started receiving the presents."

"Yes."

"How did he act toward you?"

"The same as always. A little shy; he didn't talk much."

"Did he give you any indication that he might still be interested in you?"

"No. We were only together a couple of minutes."

"Did he mention Tamura at all?"

"Well, Mr. Tamura was there too."

"Oh?"

"Yes. It was a Japanese festival, a local celebration of *Bon Odori* —the Feast of the Lanterns to commemorate the dead. A lot of people were there."

"Did you speak to Tamura?"

"Just a few words, that's all."

"And you haven't heard from Yamasaki since that day?"

Another headshake, and some more gnawing on her lower lip. She seemed to have undergone a subtle transformation in the past few minutes. The strength and determination were masked now by her anxiety and she looked young and vulnerable. I had a moronic impulse to lean over and pat her hand, but I did not give in to it. I was a detective, not a half-assed father figure.

Instead, I stood up. I had run out of questions to ask her; and this was not the time to probe for the names of other men in her life. I said, "I guess that's all for now, Mrs. Gage," and then dipped my chin at the gift box on the table. "I'd like to take the medallion with me, if you don't mind."

"Why? What are you going to do?"

"Talk to the police," I told her. "If the medallion belonged to Simon Tamura, they'll want it as evidence. I also want to find out if they've turned up Yamasaki yet and whether or not they think he had anything to do with Tamura's murder. If he did, and if he's your secret admirer, your troubles are over."

"Why would he send me the medallion after all that expensive jewelry? That doesn't make any sense."

"Maybe it makes sense to him."

She had not offered any protest, so I took the medallion out of the box, wrapped it in the tissue paper it had come in, and put it into my coat pocket. There wasn't much chance of fingerprints, because she and probably Artie had handled it, but I was careful with it just the same.

I told her not to worry—an empty reassurance that seemed to linger in the stillness like a dying echo. She didn't say anything, just kept sitting there with her hands in her lap and her eyes remote. Little girl scared, peering into the dark corners of her imagination as I went away into the rain.

Eberhardt and his new furniture were both sitting in the O'Farrell Street office when I walked in a few minutes before three. The desk was all right—simulated oak with a highly polished top and a lot of drawers—but the rest of it was the kind of white elephant stuff salesmen unload on people who don't know what they're buying. An old-fashioned swivel chair with a curved back that looked as if it had come out of somebody's attic; a couple of filing cabinets painted a mustard yellow and made out of compressed particle board so that they probably weighed about five hundred pounds each; a metal typewriter table so shaky-looking I would have been afraid to set a pen on it, much less a typewriter. He had even bought a water cooler, one of those porcelain jobs with a trough at the bottom.

The desk was over in front of the side-wall window, the one that looked out on the blank brick wall of the neighboring building. The other stuff was over there too, everything except the cooler thing; that was sitting next to the door, waiting for somebody to haul in a bottle of Alhambra Water. He'd left me the space in front of the middle two windows, under the skylight—which was decent of him, I supposed, since that space was opposite the door and would put me in the position of authority. But I still felt depressed. I had felt depressed the instant I came in.

Eberhardt was tilted back in the swivel chair with his feet up on the desk and a styrofoam cup of coffee in one hand. He waggled a shoe at me and said, "So what do you think? Do I look like a private dick?"

"You look like a dick, all right. A big one."

"You're a hoot, you are. How do you like the furniture?"

"Just dandy. Except that your file cabinets clash with the paint on the linoleum."

"Yeah, I don't like that yellow color much. Looks like baby crap. But I got a good price and I can always paint 'em white or something."

"Uh-huh."

"You think my stuff will look okay with yours?"

"Terrific. The Pinkertons'll be envious as hell."

He finished his coffee and put the cup on the floor beside him. When he learned over like that you could see the scar behind his ear where one of the bullets had lodged back in August. "What's eating you?" he said. "You getting your period, or what?"

"Now who's a hoot? No, it's this damn case I'm working on. I don't like the way it's shaping up."

"You want to talk about it?"

"Yeah, I do. We're partners now; we might as well start confiding in each other." I cocked a hip against the far corner of his desk. The light from the upside-down grappling hook overhead reflected off one of the clusters of brass balls, so that it looked like the damned things were winking at me. "Besides, I'm going to need your help."

"How so?"

"I've got to go down to the Hall and talk to Leo McFate pretty soon. I'd like you to come with me."

"Why? You're not in trouble again, are you?"

"Not with the Department."

"Who, then?"

"Maybe the Yakuza. I'm not sure."

He swung his feet off the desk and sat up. "Christ, I thought you told me—"

"Eb, when I talked to you this morning I honestly believed there wasn't any connection between Tamura's death and the case I'm working on; now I think there might be one after all. But it only concerns me indirectly. I know that, but the Yakuza might not."

"You expect me to make any sense out of that?" he said. "Start at the beginning."

So I started at the beginning and told him the whole thing in detail. He didn't interrupt; he'd been a good cop and good cops are good listeners. He stayed silent until after I'd shown him the damascene medallion. Then he spread his hands and said, "Well, it doesn't look so bad to me."

"No?"

"No. The Yakuza angle's a little dicey, sure. But the rest of it . . . I don't know, maybe you got Mrs. Gage all stirred up for nothing."

"You don't buy a connection between the medallion in the photograph and this one?"

"I can see where it's possible," he said. "But only if this Ken Yamasaki is both the killer and Mrs. Gage's unknown admirer. And even then I can't figure a motive for him swiping the medallion and sending it to her."

"Maybe he's a psycho," I said. "Pyschos only need reasons for doing things that satisfy themselves."

"Also possible. But it still looks to me like you're trying to make a big mystery out of two separate cases. Hell, you were pretty shook last night when you found Tamura; you admitted that. And you didn't take a good close look at that photograph. The two medallions might not be the same at all."

"They're the same, Eb. You'll see for yourself when you look at the photo. McFate'll have had it tagged and brought in from the baths, probably."

"Uh-huh. Now I get it."

"Get what?"

"Why you want me to go down to the Hall with you," he said. "You figure McFate might not believe this theory of yours and if he doesn't, and you're there alone, he won't let you see the photo. Or tell you how his investigation is going. But if I'm there it makes you look better, gets you some answers, and buys your way into the Property Room. Right?"

"Same old Eb," I said. "Sharp as a tack."

He told me what I could do with a sharp tack. But that and the scowl that went with it were just for show; he was enjoying himself, enjoying the idea of the two of us working together and of getting back into harness himself. Same old Eb, all right—finally. It was good to see.

So how come I still felt depressed?

"You coming to the Hall with me or not?" I asked him.

He pretended to consider it some more. Then he said, "I guess I might as well. Keep you out of any more hot water. But don't count on me having much influence now that I'm retired. Especially with McFate; we never did get along too good."

Somebody started pounding on the office door. "That'll be my furniture," I said, and got up and went to admit the storage company guys.

It took them the better part of an hour to move in my belongings: secondhand oak desk, matching chair, a trio of chrome visitors' chairs, two metal file cabinets, the blowup poster of an old *Black Mask* cover I used as a wall decoration, typewriter and stand, hot plate, and two packing boxes of miscellaneous junk. Eberhardt helped me shift the stuff around until the place looked halfway presentable. My desk covered up most of the paint stains on the linoleum, which left only the ceiling fixture and those mustard yellow file cabinets to be dealt with.

"Not too bad, is it?" Eberhardt said when we were done. "Looks kind of homey."

"Yeah," I said. It didn't look too bad at that. It was a hell of a lot more my style than the last set of offices I'd occupied, down on Drumm Street, where I'd had to put up with venetian blinds and pastel walls and a pimp-yellow phone—all because I'd had the dumb idea that I needed to project a more modern image.

Eb said, "You're not having any second thoughts, are you?" and I realized that he'd suddenly grown serious. "About the partnership, us making a go of it together?"

"What makes you ask that?"

"Well, you look kind of broody. And I want this to work out—I want it real bad."

"Same here."

"Not just for my sake. For yours too. Because . . . hell, you been a good friend and I don't want to let you down again."

"Eb . . ."

"No, I mean it. And I got to say it. If it hadn't been for you I don't know where I'd be right now. Or if I'd be anywhere. You . . . well, if I had a brother . . . ah hell, I'm no good with words," and he stuck out his hand.

I took it, and we looked at each other for a time, and I felt a little tight in the throat. And no longer depressed. The mood had peeled away all at once, like a strip of dead skin. I grinned at him finally, and he grinned back, and I said, "Come on, let's get out of here," the way they do in the TV cop shows.

We went.

Nine

Ken Yamasaki evidently had *not* been the one who'd used the samurai sword on Simon Tamura. Nor did the police have any concrete leads yet to the man who *had* used it.

Those were the first two things we found out when we got to the Hall of Justice. Not from McFate; he wasn't in yet, and he didn't show up until after five. We learned them from Jack Logan, who for years had worked under Eberhardt on the Homicide Detail and who had been promoted to lieutenant and been given Eb's old office when he retired. I knew Logan from way back, too; we'd worked together for a while when I was on the cops twenty years ago, and he'd stood up for me during that bad time a few months back when my license got suspended. The three of us sitting in the office talking was like old home wcck.

Yamasaki had been turned up this morning, at his apartment on California Street, and questioned extensively. He'd admitted to being at the bathhouse when Tamura was murdered; but he'd been in the company of two customers, both of whom had also been located and questioned and who had corroborated his story. At about nine-fifteen that night the three of them had heard screams and sounds of violence coming from Tamura's office, had gone to investigate, had got a glimpse of somebody running down the back stairs —somebody they said they couldn't identify or describe—and then had panicked and beat it out of there, along with the two other people present at the time. Yamasaki had also admitted to knowing that Tamura was a Yakuza chieftain, and to being a Yakuza runner himself; that was all McFate had been able to get out of him. He and the others had eventually been released with the usual warning to keep themselves available.

Logan seemed interested in why I was there, but in the same skeptical way Eberhardt was. Maybe Yamasaki was Haruko Gage's secret admirer and maybe he wasn't; it just didn't add up to police business, now that Yamasaki had been alibied for the time of Tamura's death. And no, as far as he knew the killer hadn't taken a medallion or anything else off Tamura's body or from anywhere in the office. All the police knew for sure was that the murder weapon had belonged to Tamura and been kept on display on the office wall; that the "perp"—the new slang term, and abbreviation of perpetrator—had gotten away through the rear entrance, leaving a trail of Tamura's blood in his wake; and that so far nobody in or out of the Yakuza claimed to know anything about the slaying. But maybe McFate had turned up something new, Logan said; he'd had a four o'clock appointment with a Japantown informant—which explained his absence from the Hall.

As for the two Japanese guys in Yamasaki's white Ford, I had no proof they were Yakuza. And even if they were, they hadn't tried to do anything to me or threatened me in any way. There was no statute on the books forbidding anybody from simply following anybody else around; they had as much right as I did to drive where they pleased. Unless they did hassle me, there wasn't much the Department could do about them.

None of that made me happy. If I'd gotten it from Logan I was sure as hell going to get the same thing from McFate. Well, if the police wouldn't pursue the medallion angle I saw no reason, as long as I was careful about it, why I shouldn't. That was what Mrs. Gage was paying me for, after all.

I badly wanted another look at that photograph, and with Eberhardt's support I might have been able to get permission from Logan. But McFate showed up just then and that put an end to the office bull session.

McFate didn't have an office; all he had was a desk in one corner of the squadroom, under a window that looked out on the freeway approach to the Bay Bridge. But you'd have thought that corner was the Chief's private sanctum, the way he held court. He told Eberhardt and me to pull up chairs and sit down, then stood over us so we'd have to look up at him. He was dressed in a sort of irridescent blue-gray suit today, with a pearl-colored shirt and a blue two-tone tie fastened by a pearl tack. The only thing that spoiled his elegant image was the scowl he wore on his face; he was not exactly over-joyed to see either of us.

"You're looking spiffy as hell these days, Leo," Eberhardt said. "The good life must be agreeing with you."

"I have no complaints. And you, Eb?"

"I got complaints, but you wouldn't be interested. You put on some weight, huh? You're a little thicker around the gut since the last time I saw you."

"I haven't put on an ounce," McFate said stiffly.

Eberhardt said, "Hunh. Must be the cut of your suit," and got out his disreputable pipe and one of those little tamper things pipe-smokers carry. Either he liked McFate even less than I did, or it was just that he had no use in general for people who thought they were better than the rest of us. Whatever the reason, he had the needle out and honed sharp.

"I take it you're not here on a social visit," McFate said. He sounded annoyed now. "State your business. I have work to do."

"I like the way you talk, Leo. 'State your business.' I like that."

"Well?"

"The Tamura case," Eberhardt said. He leaned over, scraping at his pipe bowl with the little tamper thing, and managed to dislodge ash and dottle onto McFate's pristine desktop. When he tried to blow it off he succeeded in spreading it out over more of the surface.

McFate glared at him. "Can't you be more careful with that pipe?"

"Sure, Leo. Sorry. But you know how it is with us old retired guys. We get a little clumsy sometimes."

McFate had had enough of Eberhardt; he switched his attention to me. "What about the Tamura case?" he said. "Did you forget to tell me something?"

"No," I said. "But some things have happened since last night."

"Yes? What things?"

I told him about the two guys who'd been following me in Ken Yamasaki's car. I told him about the medallion, and how I was sure

Simon Tamura had been wearing one like it in the old photograph, and outlined my theory that Tamura's death was somehow linked with Haruko Gage's secret-admirer problems. I took the medallion out of my pocket and unwrapped it and showed it to him. And when I got all done he looked me in the eye and said, "Nonsense."

I didn't say anything. But Eberhardt said, "How come, Leo? You got to admit it's possible."

"Anything is possible," McFate said. "But Simon Tamura's murder was Yakuza-related—a simple, straightforward gang killing. I'm satisfied of that."

"You are, huh? Why?"

"Because of certain facts that I've learned."

"What facts?"

"I don't think I ought to discuss them."

"Come on, Leo. Who do you think we are? Spies for the Yakuza? Undercover *Chronicle* reporters?"

"I don't find that funny," McFate said.

"That's because you got no sense of humor. What're these facts you turned up?"

McFate stayed silent for ten seconds or so, with his scowl pulling his eyes and mouth down at the corners. Then, grudgingly, he said, "Tamura was in trouble with the local gang heirarchy. It appears he had been skimming off part of the take from his *mizu shobai* operation."

"So you think the bosses put out a contract on him."

"What amounts to a contract in the Yakuza, yes. My informant was surprised it took them this long to purge him." He looked at me again. "Paid assassins don't stop to steal medallions off the men they've murdered, and they certainly don't send little mementos of their handiwork to women, anonymously or otherwise. They are not that sort of psychopathic personality."

"Maybe not," I said. "But if you're right about it being a contract hit, how do you explain those two guys following me around today?"

"In the first place, you don't know they were *kobun*—"

"What?" Eberhardt said. "What's *kobun*, Leo?"

McFate sighed in a way that said he wished to God he didn't have to suffer fools as well as knaves. "Low-level soldiers. Hired muscle."

"Uh-huh."

"And in the second place," McFate said to me, "you don't know that their reason for following you has anything to do with the Tamura homicide. It could be something else entirely." He paused. "*Is* there something you haven't told me?"

"No," I said.

"Well, then."

"What about the medallion? I'm sure this one matches the one Tamura was wearing in that photograph."

"And if it does? What does it prove? It's probably a common enough Japanese trinket."

"Haruko Gage says it isn't."

"She could be wrong, you know."

"She could also be right. At least compare this medallion to the one in the photo."

"I'll say it again," McFate said, as if he were talking to a contentious and not very bright kid. "Even if they match, what does it prove?"

"All right. So how about letting *me* compare them? For my own satisfaction."

"I don't see what purpose that would serve. Besides, you've wasted enough of my time already. I have work to do."

Eberhardt stirred. He'd been loading up his pipe again and he was getting ready to light it. "Leo, for Christ's sake unbend a little," he said. "Let him look at the photograph. You had it brought in, didn't you?"

"Of course I had it brought in."

"And it's back from the lab by now, right?"

"Yes. It's in the Property Room. But I told you—"

"So you don't even have to go along. Just call down and tell them we're coming. It's no big deal."

McFate scowled as if it was.

"Come on, Leo," Eberhardt said. "Be a *mensch.*"

McFate was a *mensch*, if just barely. He said, "As a favor, then," in reluctant tones and made the call.

When he hung up I asked him, "Are you satisfied that Ken Yamasaki isn't involved in the homicide?"

"I'm satisfied he isn't directly involved. Why?"

"I'd like your permission to talk to him."

"About what?"

"The case I'm working on. The secret admirer."

"All right. But just that. Understood?"

"Understood."

Eberhardt had finished lighting his pipe with one of the little wooden matches he uses. He made a show of looking around for an ashtray that wasn't there, then threw the match in the general direction of the wastebasket. But his aim was off by about ten feet: the match landed in the middle of McFate's upholstered chair and lay there smoldering.

McFate made a wounded noise when the match landed, lunged at the chair, picked the match up, and hurled it into the wastebasket. "For God's sake!" he said. "Can't you be more careful?"

"Sorry, Leo," Eberhardt said blandly. He got to his feet, and I followed suit. "I won't bring my pipe next time I stop by for a chat."

We left McFate looking exasperated and walked out of the squad-room to the elevators. I said, "Now you know what it's like on the other side of the fence."

"Yeah. And I think I'm going to like it on your side." He grinned a little. "Especially when Leo's around."

"You really did a number on him in there. How come?"

"Like I told him, he's got no sense of humor. I always did enjoy getting a rise out of him."

"Is that the only reason?"

He gave me a sidewise look. "What do you think?"

"I think McFate is an asshole."

"Bingo," he said.

We rode the elevator down to the Property Room, where the SFPD keeps evidence, weapons, and confiscated items of all types, among other things. The sergeant in charge was a friend of Eberhardt's, and he was the one who'd taken McFate's call, so we had no trouble getting through security. The sergeant brought the photograph out and stood by while Eb and I bent over one of the tables, peering at it.

The medallions seemed to match, all right, when I laid the one I'd gotten from Haruko Gage next to the one in the print. As grainy as the old photo was, the blowup of it made the medallion and its odd design clearly visible.

Eberhardt grunted. "So they're the same," he said. "I hate to
sound like McFate, but what *does* it prove?"

"I don't know yet."

I studied the photo itself for a time. The three men, Simon
Tamura in the middle, their arms around one another and their faces
split by wide grins. The wire-mesh fence behind them, and the
distant, blurred buildings beyond. None of that told me anything.

Who were the other two men? I wondered. And then I turned
the photograph over and slipped it out of its broken frame, and I
had my answer. Simon Tamura was one of those people who write
information on the backs of photos; there were some Japanese cha-
racters drawn in ink, and also some words in English. The English
words said: *With Sanjiro Masaoka and Kazuo Hama—1945.*

I wrote the names down in my notebook. Then I turned the photo
over again and looked at it a while longer, fixing the two faces that
flanked Tamura's in my mind. Then I said to Eb and to the sergeant,
"Okay, that should do it," and a couple of minutes later we were on
our way out of the building.

Eberhardt asked, "What next, mastermind?"

"Nothing, today." It was six o'clock and dark and still raining; I'd
had enough of today as far as work went. "Tomorrow I go see Ken
Yamasaki. And run a check on those two names in the photo; there
might be an angle there if Masaoka and Hama are still alive and still
living around here."

"Uh-huh. You sure you're not running off half-cocked on this
thing?"

"No," I said, "I'm not sure."

"But that won't stop you from going ahead, right?"

"If it ever does I'll get out of the business."

"I figured. Anything else you want me to do?"

"I guess not. I'll take it from here, Eb. Thanks."

I dropped him at his car on O'Farrell Street and drove on up to
Pacific Heights. There was no sign of the white Ford, or of any other
car full of Japanese, in the vicinity of my building. I circled the block
a couple of times to make sure. So maybe they'd given up on me,
after the little episode out by China Beach this morning. I hoped
so; I did not want to be anybody important or even interesting as
far as the Yakuza was concerned.

The first thing I did when I entered the flat was to check the telephone book for a local listing on either Sanjiro Masaoka or Kazuo Hama. No luck; it wasn't going to be that easy.

My answering machine had one message on it—from Jeanne Emerson, asking again if I would please call her as soon as possible. No, I would not please call her as soon as possible. I would call her tomorrow—maybe. On the other hand, if I ignored her she might just go away; and that might be the best solution for all of us. Especially for me, craven coward that I was when it came to women.

I called Kerry instead and asked her if I could come over and tell her about my day and maybe continue our discussion on primitive mating habits. She said, "I know you, you've got lust in your heart," and I said, "Yup," and she said, "All right, then, I'll risk it. Come ahead. I'll see what I can find for dinner."

What she'd found for dinner, I discovered when I got there, was a tuna fish salad with hardboiled eggs and some crackers and an apple for dessert. She saw me looking at it and told me to quit making faces and sit down and eat. I obeyed; I would have eaten anything right then, including the asparagus fern she had hanging in one corner of the dining area.

Over coffee I gave her a rundown of my day. We discussed matters for a while, to no particular conclusion. Then I made a fire with a Presto-log and we sat on the couch and watched the rain patter down outside her picture window, distorting the lights of the city. The fire and the rain made me drowsy and amorous at the same time. So I showed her a few of my primitive moves, the preliminary ones, and she suggested I show her the rest of my repertoire in the bedroom. We got up and walked in there holding hands.

Well, it should have been a terrific finale after all that buildup. It should have been passion and excitement and atavism and fulfillment, followed by tenderness and languor and gentle touching. It should have been a lot of things like that, but it wasn't any of them. It wasn't any damned thing at all.

I fell asleep waiting for her to come out of the bathroom in her sexy black negligee.

Ten

I didn't get any loving in the morning, either. Kerry was already up and in the shower when I woke up at seven-thirty; I remembered groggily that even though it was Saturday, she had an early meeting at Bates and Carpenter. I lurched into the bathroom with the idea of getting something started in the shower, but by the time I got there she was on her way out. I made a grab at all that pink and glowing flesh; she swatted me with her towel, hard enough to sting.

"Well, well," she said, "the big lover's alive after all."

"Ah, hell, I'm sorry I fell asleep. But I had a rough day. Why didn't you wake me up?"

"I tried to wake you up. You've probably got bruises all over you from me trying to wake you up."

I made another grab for her, and she smacked me again with the towel. "I don't have time now, Don Juan," she said. "You had your chance."

I said something petulant.

"Go weigh yourself," she said.

"What? What kind of suggestion is that?"

"*Weigh*, you idiot, not lay. Go weigh yourself on my scale. Let's see how much weight you've lost so far."

Grumbling, I went and stepped on the scale. It was one of those fancy jobs with frilly covers that women have and I felt foolish standing on it all naked and hairy. Two hundred and twenty-seven pounds, it said. Give or take half a pound.

"Down about three," I said over my shoulder.

"Is that all?"

"That's all. I been starving myself for two weeks for a lousy three pounds."

"Well, it takes time," she said. "You'll lose a lot all at once. It always works that way."

"Yeah," I said, "sure," and got off the scale and into the shower. I thought about three rashers of bacon and flapjacks with maple syrup and a whole canteloupe. Then I got out and dried myself and dressed and Kerry served me two softboiled eggs and half a grapefruit for breakfast. I felt a little like bawling.

She left for the agency at eight-twenty, while I was still working on my coffee and feeling deprived. I was in no hurry myself; I didn't want to go knocking on doors before nine o'clock, and I couldn't get in touch with Harry Fletcher at the DMV before nine-thirty. I picked up one of the pulps I'd loaned Kerry and tried to read a story by William Campbell Gault, one of the best of the old pulpsters; but I was too hungry and restless to enjoy it. I got up and paced around instead, finishing my coffee.

Kerry's apartment is big—two bedrooms, one of them converted into an office; living room, dining area, kitchen, two bathrooms, and a utility porch. Among other features, it has modernistic furniture with lots of chrome and sharp angles and whitish, tweedy-looking upholstery; massive paintings of the abstract impressionist type, emphasis on blacks and whites and oranges; an antique brass double bed, the only nonmodern furnishing in the place; and lots of bookshelves full of all sorts of fiction and nonfiction, because Kerry is a reader like me and has much more catholic tastes. I liked all of those things—they were warm and comfortable and individual and a little unconventional, just as Kerry herself was. The only thing I didn't like about the place, in fact, was that she kept framed photographs of her parents in the bedroom, and it always seemed as though Ivan the Terrible was watching us make love and maybe thinking up evil curses to wither my immortal soul. He *was* an expert on the occult, after all.

Without Kerry there, the apartment felt incomplete. It also made me feel doubly deprived—but then, I only had myself to blame for my sexual frustration. Falling asleep like that . . . my God! The next step was probably lapses of memory and eccentric behavior, and the one after that would be commitment to a home where a battery of nurses could take turns wiping the drool off my chin.

Time to go to work, I thought. Busy hands are happy hands and all that crap. I put the coffee cup in the kitchen, rinsed it out, got my coat, locked the apartment door behind me with Kerry's spare key, walked downstairs and outside, started toward where I had left my car—and came to a sudden standstill.

Across the street and fifty yards down the block was a familiar white Ford with two Japanese guys sitting in it.

It made me more angry than anything else. The first thing I thought was that they'd followed me here from my flat last night, even though I'd been watching and hadn't spotted them. Then I remembered that Kerry's name had been in the news story about Tamura's death, and that she was listed in the telephone book. After I'd surprised them yesterday, they must have switched tactics and gone to tail *her* instead.

I put my hands in my overcoat pockets so the two guys wouldn't see me clenching them. Then I walked over there, not doing it in any hurry. It wasn't raining at the moment, although the sky was heavy with clouds, and I could see them both clearly through the windshield. They didn't do anything except watch me in return—didn't even move their heads.

When I came up onto the sidewalk in front of them I saw that the driver's window was rolled down. So I kept on going until I was abreast of it and then stopped and squatted down and looked in at them. The one with the nose like a blob of putty was behind the wheel today; he stared back at me with an expression as blank as an erased slate. The other one ran a finger slowly and rhythmically over his mustache and looked straight ahead, trancelike, as if he were a Buddhist monk trying to achieve Nirvana.

"Something I can do for you boys?" I said.

Neither of them responded. The putty-nosed one kept on staring through me; I might have been a lamppost or a fire hydrant, or not there at all.

"Yesterday morning, out by China Beach," I said. "You followed me there and I spotted you and got your license number. Remember?"

Silence.

"I don't like to be followed," I said. "And I especially don't like having friends of mine followed. If you want something from me, suppose you just cut out the crap and get right down to it."

Silence. The putty-nosed one turned his head slightly and I saw his eyes flicker to the CB radio unit mounted under the dash.

"Go ahead," I said, "call up whoever you're working for. Tell him I'm here waiting. Tell him to come talk to me so we can get this business finished."

More silence. The other guy quit stroking his mustache, but that was all that happened. They just sat there. I had the thought that if I reached in and smacked one or the other they wouldn't even try to retaliate. Not without orders.

There wasn't anything more for me to say. I straightened, put my back to the Ford, and recrossed the street to where my car was parked. When I got inside I rolled the window down and adjusted the side-view mirror so I could watch them while I started the engine and let it warm up. The putty-nosed guy was talking into the CB microphone; I could see the handset and the cord even from this distance.

Ten to one they get the same orders they got yesterday, I thought. Cease and desist—for the time being.

But I would have lost the bet. Damned if they didn't pull out behind me as I drove off, and damned if they didn't follow me all the way to my flat in Pacific Heights.

The Department of Motor Vehicles was open half a day on Saturday. I got through to Harry Fletcher at nine-forty, spelled out the two names that had been on the back of the photograph, told him their approximate ages, and asked him to get me addresses for all California residents who matched up. Neither name seemed particularly common, although I was no expert on Japanese nomenclature. Fletcher wasn't either; he said to give him an hour, just in case.

I decided there were better things to do with that hour than hang around the flat. I checked the answering machine, discovered that nobody had called me since last evening, and went back out to my car. When I glanced up at the rear-view mirror after half a block, the white Ford was right there in my wake again.

I considered trying a few maneuvers to shake them. But I was too old for fast driving games; and I would have had to detour all the way downtown to try shaking them in traffic. Besides which, they would only show up at my flat again later on. Or worse, go bother Kerry again. The best thing to do was to let them tag along and see that I wasn't doing anything sinister or thrilling, and maybe that would convince them to go away. If not, I would have to find some way to deal with them later on.

So I drove straight out California Street without paying much attention to the Ford. Number 2610 was an old, beige, stucco apartment house a few blocks this side of Children's Hospital—the kind with a wide front stoop and fire escapes zig-zagging down its facade like livid scars. There was a bus zone in front of it; I parked there illegally. The two *kobun* drove on by, turned the corner, and stopped alongside a fire hydrant, which was even more illegal.

I went up onto the front stoop of 2610 and hunted among the mailbox nameplates until I found *K. Yamasaki, Apt. 7.* I pushed the button next to that one and kept my finger on it for fifteen seconds or so. Nothing happened, except that an elderly Japanese lady came down the flight of stairs inside, opened the door, and stepped out.

"Excuse me, ma'am," I said. "Do you know Ken Yamasaki?"

She gave me one of those looks people reserve for strangers who might also be insurance or household accessory salesmen: half wary, half blank. "Yes?" she said.

"He doesn't seem to be in. Would you happen to know where I can find him?"

"Yes?" she said.

"Where would that be?"

"Yes?"

"Ma'am . . . do you speak English?"

"Yes?"

"Terrific. Sorry to have bothered you." I started down the steps, paused, and said, "Uh, *sayonara.*"

"Yes," she said, without the question mark this time, and bobbed her head and grinned as she followed after me.

I was pretty slow this morning: It didn't occur to me until I was getting into the car that she probably did speak English and had been putting me on the whole time.

I stopped at a Chevron station out near Park Presidio Drive, and while an attendent fed the car I went to the phone booth nearby and rang up the DMV again. There were two sixtyish Kazuo Hamas living in California, Fletcher told me, only one up here in the northern part of the state; that one's residence was Hama Egg Ranch, Rainsville Road, Petaluma. Petaluma was close to San Francisco—about forty miles away to the north. The other Kazuo Hama lived in Orange County, in some town I had never heard of. I took down his address too.

The DMV records showed a single Sanjiro Masaoka: 72 West Point Avenue, Princeton. Which was even closer to the city, Princeton being a small fishing village snuggled up to the larger community of Half Moon Bay, some twenty-five miles south on Highway One.

I thanked Fletcher, promised him a couple of bottles of Johnnie Walker Red Label—he wouldn't take money from me because he said it made him feel dishonest—and went back and ransomed the car. When I left the station I swung over to Geary and drove out to the Great Highway and then pointed the car south toward Highway One. I didn't have anything better to do, the rain was still holding off, and Princeton was a good place to get a seafood lunch, if nothing else. Or it would have been if I hadn't had my unwanted company.

The white Ford stayed behind me all the way down.

Eleven

The road that led into Princeton angled off Highway One and skirted the edge of the small Half Moon Bay airfield. There wasn't much to the central part of the village—an old inn, a grocery store, a couple of restaurants, and some craft stores that catered to tourists. Straight ahead was a communal pier and the white-flecked water of Pillar Point Harbor, where a bunch of fishing boats rocked at anchor and geometrically laid out rock jetties marked the channels.

Off to the west were a fish-processing plant and a boatyard and three or four square blocks of private houses. I turned that way in front of the inn. All the rough-paved streets were named after colleges; West Point Avenue was one of the longest and easy enough to find. I crawled along it in deference to its potholes, past a variety of houses ranging from comfortable old frame to tumbledown shacks; past bright green, fieldlike lots and boggy yards full of boats large and small, some up on drydock davits and some that were little more than rotting hulks.

Number 72 was near the inner sweep of the harbor—a smallish two-story shingled house painted box-car red, shaded in front by a line of cypress trees and enclosed by a mossy woodstake fence. In the yard behind the fence I could see stacks of cordwood and old tree stumps, and the rusted skeleton of a bus that appeared to serve now as a shed or workshop. The bus had once belonged to a tribe of hippies, judging from the remnants of flower decals that decorated its sides; it sat there like a relic from some ancient and curious civilization. And in a way, maybe it was.

I parked in front, between a pair of rain puddles that resembled miniature ponds. The air had a sharp salt tang mingled with the smell of ozone; it was going to rain again pretty soon. As I approached the gate I could see that all of the house's facing windows, downstairs and upstairs both, had shades drawn over them. It gave the place a closed-up, abandoned look.

The gate was latched; I reached over and opened it and went inside along a short muddy path. The porch stairs made little popping, creaking noises as I climbed them. Except for the distant racket of gulls, those pops and creaks were the only sounds in the heavy quiet.

On the front door was one of those old-fashioned doorbells that you have to twist to ring, like winding up an alarm clock. Nobody answered the ratchety summons. I tried it again, with the same nonresults, and decided Sanjiro Masaoka was somewhere else this morning and that maybe one of his neighbors could tell me where that might be. I turned from the door, took one step, and immediately quit moving again.

There was a dog down at the bottom of the porch stairs, sitting on its haunches and staring at me with bright yellow eyes.

It was a Doberman and it was big and it looked menacing as hell, even though it wasn't doing anything except sitting there. The hackles went up on my neck. Usually I get along all right with dogs, as long as they're kept on leashes and not allowed to crap all over sidewalks and people's lawns. But a Doberman is something else again. Dobermans stir up some sort of primitive fear in me; I don't like them one bit and I steer clear of them whenever our paths happen to cross.

Neither of us moved. We just kept looking at each other for what seemed like a long time. Where the hell had he come from? I'd closed the gate behind me, so he hadn't wandered in off the street. Which meant he'd been on the property the whole time, somewhere out back. Which in turn probably meant that he belonged here— Sanjiro Masaoka's dog—and if *he* belonged here, he knew *I* didn't.

I worked up some saliva, swallowed it to lubricate my throat, and said, "Easy, boy. Easy. Nice dog," to see what would happen.

The Doberman pricked up his ears. Then he began to growl low in his throat. Otherwise he didn't move; his little stub of a tail was as stiff as if it was welded onto his rump.

Oh, fine, I thought. Dogs that growled instead of barked and didn't wag their tails were dangerous dogs. So why hadn't Masaoka put out a BEWARE OF DOG sign so people like me wouldn't wander in and maybe get themselves chewed on?

I looked away from the Doberman, out toward the street. The white Ford had pulled up about fifty yards behind my car, in front of a weathered neighboring house with a screened-in front porch, and the two Japanese guys were staring in my direction. I had a momentary impulse to call out to them. But even if they had been inclined to help me, which they no doubt weren't, any loud noise like a shout might set the Doberman off. You never knew with high-strung dogs like that, even if they were trained, what was liable to trigger them.

He quit growling after another few seconds, but he didn't take his eyes off me. I kept looking around for some avenue of escape or somebody to come along, but the former didn't exist and the latter didn't seem to either. The muscles in my neck and back and bad arm began to cramp up with tension. I met the dog's gaze again and tried some man-staring-down-dumb-beast stuff. It didn't work; he had a more forceful will than I did when it came to confrontations like this.

A good five minutes went by. The Doberman kept staring, the Japanese guys kept staring, the cramps got worse, and I began to grow more irritated than anxious. The hell with it, I thought finally, and I took a slow, careful step toward the stairs.

The Doberman got up, spread his forepaws, and commenced snarling.

I froze in place. Those yellow eyes were all hot now and full of what I took to be bloodlight. I forgot about being brave and annoyed and got anxious again. Christ, how long was I going to have to stand here before somebody rescued me or the goddamn dog decided to attack?

As it turned out, I had to stand there worrying about three more minutes. Then the screen door at the weathered house next door opened and a woman came out and down her porch steps. She stopped at the foot of them, put her hands on her hips, and peered at the white Ford. Pretty soon she moved in a purposeful way to her front gate and said something that I didn't catch to the two *kobun*. But it must have been a threat—to call the county cops on them for loitering in front of her house, maybe—because it wasn't long before the Ford's engine revved up and the car pulled out and went past me and the Masaoka house. Not far, though; it turned the corner at the nearest intersection and angled off onto the verge again.

The woman had also followed the Ford's progress and that allowed her to notice me. She peered in my direction the way she had peered at the Ford, then walked out through her gate and came down the street and stopped before Masaoka's gate. She was around sixty, sun-cured and bony and gray-haired, wearing a tattered sweater with suede elbow patches. A tough old bird. Which suited me just fine.

"Hey, you," she said. To me, not to the Doberman. "What're you doing in there?"

What does it look like I'm doing? I thought. I'm standing here waiting for the Hound of the Baskervilles to tear out my throat. But I said quietly, so as not to stir up the dog, "I came to see Mr. Masaoka on a business matter. There's nobody home except Fido here."

"Oh," she said in a funny kind of voice. Then she said, "His name's Tomodachi. That means 'friend' in Japanese."

"Yeah," I said, "sure."

"What'd you do, just walk in on him?"

"I didn't see him. Or any Beware of Dog sign."

"Used to be a sign. Some kids stole it."

"Look, ma'am, you suppose you could do something about getting me out of here? I don't like the way he keeps staring at me."

"Well, he *can* be vicious sometimes," she said. "Tomodachi! Get away! Leave the man alone!"

The Doberman turned his head and gave her a quick look. But he didn't obey; he swung his gaze back to me and snarled some more and shuffled his front paws. I got ready to defend myself, but nothing happened.

"Damn," the woman said. "I never could talk to him. Or get near him unless Sanjiro was around. Might be a way, though. I'll be right back; you stay where you are."

Lady, I thought, where am I going to go?

She trotted away to her own property, disappeared inside her house for about two minutes, reappeared, and came hurrying back to the Masaoka gate. When she neared it I could see what it was she was holding in one hand: a couple of beaten-up old tennis balls.

"Tomodachi likes to play ball," she told me. "He likes it more than just about anything."

"More than attacking strangers, I hope."

"I'll try to get him to fetch," she said. "Then I'll open the gate and you make a run for it."

"Like a world-class sprinter," I said.

"Ball!" she said loudly to the Doberman. "Ball, Tomodachi! Let's play ball!"

It got his attention. His ears pricked up again, his head came around, and his tongue rolled out of his mouth like a flag unfurling. The woman showed him one of the tennis balls, kept on chattering at him until she succeeded in getting him half turned around and dividing his attention between the two of us. At which point she pulled her arm back and yelled "Fetch!" and uncorked a throw Willie Mays would have been proud of, over toward where the tree stumps were piled.

The Doberman wheeled, she got ready to yank open the gate, I

got ready to run like hell . . . and the dog ran five feet and stopped
and came back and snarled at me some more.

The woman said, "Shit." Which were my sentiments exactly.

So we had to go through the whole thing again, only longer this
time, like extended foreplay, in order to get the dog all hot and
bothered over the idea of playing fetch. She teased him with words,
juggled the ball from one hand to the other, pretended three or four
times that she was going to throw it. The last time she cocked her
arm, he scooted away a few feet in anticipation; he was as ready then
as he would ever be. And so was I.

The woman glanced at me, and I nodded, and she hauled her arm
back again and yelled "Fetch!" and let fly, in the general direction
of the hippie-relic bus. The Doberman and I both took off at the
same time. I sailed down over the four porch steps without touching
any of them, stumbled when I landed, saw that the woman had the
gate open, saw that the dog had put on the brakes and was starting
to twist back toward me with his fangs bared, caught my balance,
and charged ahead slipping and sliding on the muddy path. I got to
the opening just as the dog launched himself at my backside, and
went galumphing through. The woman slammed the gate shut; the
Doberman must have barreled right into it because I heard him yelp.
But if he got his dignity wounded, so did I: I had been running so
fast that I couldn't slow down soon enough and I caromed off the
side of my car, did a crazy pirouette to one side, tripped, and
splashed down into one of the rain puddles.

I said some things that ought to have blistered the paint off the
car. The woman didn't even flinch; she'd come over to the edge of
the puddle and was trying not to laugh at me. "Are you all right?"
she asked.

"Yeah, I'm just dandy." I got onto my feet and sloshed to the car
and leaned against the front fender. The Doberman was making
lemme-at-him noises and glaring at me through the wood-stake
fence; I glared back at him in the same malevolent way. Dogs.
Phooey.

The woman said, "Come on over to my place. I'll let you use a
towel."

"Thanks. And thanks for the rescue."

"Always glad to be neighborly," she said. She was still trying not to laugh at me.

We went to her house and she gave me the towel and the use of her bathroom to repair some of the damage to my suit. When I came out she had a cup of coffee for me. She said her name was Ethel Pinkham, grimaced to let me know she hated both ends of it, and told me to call her Pink. Everyone did, she said, and went on to explain that when her late husband was alive he'd been Pink One and she'd been Pink Two. I gave her my name, but not what I did for a living or what my business was with Masaoka. And she didn't ask.

She said, "Poor Tomodachi. I been feeding him—scraps over the fence; he won't let me come in the yard either. But he needs care and a new home. One of Sanjiro's cousins was supposed to come pick him up three days ago. If she doesn't get here by tomorrow morning I'm calling the SPCA."

"I don't follow, Pink. Why does the dog need a new home?"

"Oh, that's right—you don't know. Otherwise you wouldn't have come looking for Sanjiro."

"Don't know what?"

"He's dead," she said. "Been dead eight days now."

It took me a couple of seconds to absorb that. Then I said, "How did he die?"

"Some kind of fall. Nobody knows for sure."

"Where did it happen? His house?"

"No. Out toward the point. He'd been abaloneing by himself, like usual, and he must have fallen off the rocks. One of those freak accidents."

"This happened eight days ago, you say?"

She nodded. "Early in the morning. Couple of kids found him wedged in amongst the rocks. Hadn't been dead more than a few hours at the time."

"Was he married?"

"Widower. His wife died three . . . four years back."

"So he lived alone?"

"Just him and Tomodachi."

"What about this cousin? Does she live around here?"

"Nope. Over in Fresno."

"Where she and Masaoka close, do you know?"

"Sanjiro wasn't close to anybody after his wife died," Pink said. "Took it pretty hard and kept to himself after that. Hardly ever had any visitors or left the village. That's why I was so surprised to see you over there today."

"You didn't know him well, then?"

"Well as anybody around here. We were neighbors twelve years. His wife Yoshiko and I used to take tea together sometimes. Nice woman, real pretty. She died of cancer. He carried her picture with him all the time in a little gold locket."

"Locket? What sort of locket?"

"Little gold one, like I said. Shaped like a heart."

"With a pearl on one side?"

"Why, that's right. How did you—?"

"I've seen lockets like that," I said quickly. "In fact, I've been planning to buy one for my wife." But I was thinking: First the medallion and now the gold locket—both of which could have come off men newly dead. What in the name of Christ is going on here?

I wanted to ask her if Masaoka's locket had been missing from his body when he was found, but I doubted it was something she'd know. And it was the kind of provocative question that might arouse her suspicions and lead to difficulties. Instead I asked, "Did Masaoka ever mention any friends in San Francisco?"

"No, not that I recall."

"Does the name Simon Tamura mean anything to you?"

"Let's see—Tamura. Is kind of familiar, come to think on it. Didn't I read something about a Tamura in the papers recently?"

I did not want to get into that with her, either. I said, "But you don't remember Masaoka using that name?"

"Can't say I do."

"How about a man named Kazuo Hama?"

"Hama, Hama. Nope."

"This fellow Hama might live in Orange County. Did Masaoka ever mention knowing anyone down there?"

"Nope."

"Hama might also be a rancher in Petaluma," I said.

She shook her head. "Only rancher from Petaluma I ever heard tell of," she said, "was a shirtail cousin of my late husband's. He was an alcoholic—the shirttail cousin, I mean. Set himself on fire one night while he was drunk and burned down his house and barn and touched off his cornfield when he went running through it. Pink One thought that was the funniest thing he'd ever heard when he found out. Me, I'm not so sure."

I asked her if Masaoka had ever spoken of Haruko Gage or Ken Yamasaki, and she answered negatively both times. She was curious now over all the questions; I could see it in her eyes. Which made it time for me to leave. So I said I'd better get home and change out of my wet clothes before I caught cold, and Pink agreed that that was a good idea.

"Take some peppermint tea laced with rum and honey," she said. "Best thing in the world to fight off a cold."

The thought of peppermint tea laced with rum and honey made my throat close up. But I said, "Thanks, I'll fix up a cup when I get home."

"You do that."

We went outside together. When I looked off to the east I could see the white Ford still parked around the corner of the next intersecting street. Pink noticed it too. She said, "You know those Japanese in that car over there?"

"No," I said.

"Me neither. They were parked out front while you were at Sanjiro's." She gave me a speculative look. "You sure you don't know 'em?"

"Positive. Maybe they're tourists."

"Don't look like any tourists I ever saw."

"I'd better go," I said. "Thanks again, Pink."

"Don't mention it. Watch out for mean dogs from now on." She favored me with an amused grin. "Rain puddles, too."

I returned the grin, walked out of her yard and up to my car. The Doberman came pounding off the porch of the Masaoka house and stuck his snout between two of the fence stakes and snarled at me again. But that was all right; I didn't hate him any more, or even dislike him. I knew how it was to be lonely.

I got out the blanket I keep in the trunk and spread it over the front seat to keep my damp pants off the upholstery. Then I started the car and drove down to the near corner and made the turn past the white Ford.

The two stone-faced *kobun* raised their hands and waggled their fingers in my direction—the first animation either of them had shown. The bastards had seen me run away from the Doberman and fall into the rain puddle, and it was their way of laughing at me, too.

Twelve

I drove straight back to San Francisco. Even if I had felt like stopping in Princeton for lunch, which I didn't, I couldn't have done it in my damp suit. I needed to get home and change clothes before I did anything else.

On the way I did plenty of ruminating. The fact of Sanjiro Masaoka's sudden death made two of the three men in that photograph dead of unnatural causes within a week of each other. Coincidence? Maybe; things like that happen sometimes. But what about the medallion? What about the gold locket? It seemed to be stretching coincidence a little too far that Haruko Gage would have received a locket exactly like Masaoka carried the day after he died, and a medallion exactly like the one Simon Tamura wore the day after *he* died.

But if it wasn't coincidence, then what the hell was it? A pair of murders, with Masaoka having been pushed or clubbed out on those rocks? Then where was the motive for the two slayings? If somebody was bent on eliminating males in Haruko's life, her husband Artie was the obvious first choice. Besides which, both Masaoka and Simon Tamura had been in their sixties, and she had claimed not to know Tamura very well.

It was possible there was some connection between her and Masaoka. Or her and Kazuo Hama. And what about Kazuo Hama? Could *he* be responsible for the deaths of Masaoka and Tamura? If so, why? And even if there was a connection between Hama and Haruko, or Masaoka and Haruko, I still couldn't conjure up a motive that would fit the facts I had dug up.

Why were the locket and the medallion sent to Haruko? And

what about the other presents she'd received? Had they also once belonged to men now dead?

And where did the Yakuza fit into all of the above?

It was the screwiest business I'd ever come up against. A lot of the pieces kept cropping up, but I could not seem to get them together so they amounted to anything. For that matter, I couldn't even get a good grasp on them individually. It was like trying to load a thermometer with beads of quicksilver, without the proper tools: every time you tried to pick up one of the beads, it squirted away from you.

My watch said it was one-thirty when I entered my building. No mail in the box downstairs, no messages on the answering machine upstairs. I went into the bathroom and took a hot shower and ate some Vitamin C capsules as a precautionary measure; the last thing I needed right now was to come down with a bad head cold.

When I was dressed again I rang up Sonoma County Directory Assistance and found out the number of the Hama Egg Ranch in Petaluma. But all I got, when I dialed the number, were a dozen unanswered rings.

I called the Gage house to find out what Haruko had to say about Sanjiro Masaoka and Kazuo Hama. But I didn't find out anything there either; she wasn't home. Artie the wimp told me she'd gone shopping and he wasn't sure when she'd be back—around three, maybe. Then he asked me if I had any news. I said no, and he said he wasn't surprised and hung up on me.

Artie, I thought as I put the receiver down, I ought to introduce you to Leo McFate, Artie. A couple of assholes like you two ought to get along fine.

I looked in the refrigerator. The only thing worth eating was a carrot, so I ate one, feeling like Bugs Bunny in a Loony Tunes cartoon, and washed it down with a can of V-8 juce. My mood, by this time, was none too genial. If I hung around here doing nothing I would be climbing the walls inside half an hour. Instead I put on one of my dry overcoats and left the flat again.

So, naturally, the rain decided to start up as I was walking to where I'd parked the car, and I got wet again. And if I needed anything else to cheer me up, the white Ford was there in my rear-view mirror as I drove away.

I headed out California and eventually stopped, as I had this morning, in the bus zone in front of Ken Yamasaki's apartment house. The Ford repeated its earlier procedure too: went around the corner and parked by the fire hydrant. I got out and climbed the stairs to the stoop and pushed the button next to Yamasaki's name and waited. And kept on waiting. No answering buzz. No nothing.

"Goddamn it!" I said out loud, and a guy passing by on the sidewalk gave me a funny look, pulled his umbrella down lower like a shield, and began to walk faster.

I got out one of my business cards and wrote on the back of it: *Call me immediately. Important.* I pushed the card through the little slot on the front of Yamasaki's mailbox, went back down the steps, and kept on going past my car until I reached the Ford. Behind the rain-streaked window glass, the two *kobun* peered at me as stoically as ever. I made a motion for the mustached one to wind down his window; he stared out at me without complying. I managed to control my anger. Instead of yanking open the door and hauling him out and yelling into his face, I leaned down and said just loud enough for both of them to hear, "Tell your boss I want to talk to him. Tell him to make it quick. And tell him I want you two off my tail by tomorrow morning. Or else I won't be responsible for what happens."

Blank stares.

Back in my car, I made an illegal U-turn in the middle of the street and drove back to Pacific Heights. The two of them tagged along after me as if nothing had happened.

I was still steaming when I came into the flat. I banged some coffee water down on the stove, then tried again to get through to the Hama Egg Ranch in Petaluma. Still no answer. I got Orange County information on the phone, wrote down the number the operator gave me for the second Kazuo Hama, and called him up. He was home; he was also the wrong Kazuo Hama. He worked for Japan Air Lines, he said, had only been in this country eight years, and had never heard of either Sanjiro Masaoka or Simon Tamura.

It was almost three o'clock by then; I rang up the Gage house to find out if Haruko had returned. She had. But when I asked her about Masaoka and Hama, she claimed not to know or have heard of either man.

"Did you ever date any older men?" I asked her. "Men in their late fifties or sixties?"

"No, of course not. I don't have a father fixation."

"Nobody at all over fifty?"

Nobody at all over forty," she said. "I don't understand. Is there some reason you think my secret admirer is over fifty?"

"Not exactly, no."

"Then why ask me that question. And who are those men—Masaoka and Hama?"

"People whose names have come up," I said. "Friends of Simon Tamura's."

Silence for a time. Finally she said, "That again—the murder. You still think there's some connection between Mr. Tamura and me, don't you?"

"I don't know what I think right now."

"But what if there *is* some connection? What if it's the same man and he decided to . . ." She didn't finish the sentence, but it was plain enough what the rest of the words would have been.

"That's not going to happen," I said.

"Maybe we should call the police."

"I've already talked it over with the police."

"You have? What did they say?"

"They don't think you have anything to worry about either." It was time to change the subject, and quickly. I said, "You know a lot of people in the Japanese community, Mrs. Gage. Is there anyone who could give me some detailed information on the Yakuza?"

"Well," she said, and stopped, and then said, "Yes, I suppose Mike Kanaya could."

"Who's Mike Kanaya?"

"A reporter for the *Hokubei Mainichi*. That's a bilingual newspaper published in Japantown—half in English and half in Japanese."

"Do you know him well enough to arrange a meeting for me?"

"Yes. But I don't know if he'll agree to talk about the Yakuza. It isn't a subject Japanese discuss openly with *gaijin*—with non-Japanese."

"See what you can do, Mrs. Gage. It might be important."

"All right. When do you want to see Mike?"

"As soon as possible."

She said she would try to get in touch with Mike Kanaya and call me back after she talked to him, and we rang off. I went out to the kitchen, where I found that most of the coffee water had boiled away; I'd forgotten I had put it on. This was not my day. I couldn't remember, in fact, the last day that had been mine. I put some more water in the pot, the pot back on the stove, and sat down at the kitchen table to wait and brood.

The waiting got me a cup of too-strong coffee; the brooding got me nothing. I got up after awhile and paced around and watched the rain roll down the glass in the bay windows like tears down mourning faces. Then I went into the bedroom and tried to call the Hama Egg Ranch again, without any more luck than before. I debated trying Kerry's number—she'd expected to be home from Bates and Carpenter around three—but I didn't want to tie up the line until Haruko Gage called back.

It was getting dark when Haruko finally did call. She'd got in touch with Mike Kanaya, she said, and he was willing to talk to me; but the soonest he could make it was tomorrow noon, because of business obligations today and tonight and family obligations tomorrow morning. I sighed a little and said all right. Kanaya had suggested meeting at a Japan Center *sushi* bar; I agreed to that too.

Not being able to see Kanaya until tomorrow pretty much left me with a free evening. It was too late to drive up to Petaluma, especially on a blind lead and with nobody home at the Hama ranch. And there wasn't any other business I could conduct this late either. What I might as well do, I thought, was call up Kerry and invite her over for dinner. That way, we could go to bed early and I could get at least one of my little problems taken care of.

So I dialed her number, and she was home. She was also tired and grouchy and coming down with something, and all she wanted to do, she said, was crawl into bed. I offered to come over and crawl into bed with her, but she didn't think that was a good idea. She wasn't in the mood for sex or even companionship, she said. She just needed to sleep, she said. Call me tomorrow and we'll see how I feel then, she said. Good-bye, she said.

I put the phone down. I looked at the four walls and thought again about climbing them. I got my coat and hat and went out into the rain.

I had a big evening for myself. Yes I did. I ate a low-calorie meal at a café on Chestnut Street, after which I went to a double feature at one of the revival houses downtown, after which I drove home and went to bed.

The food was awful. So were the movies. And so was sleeping alone.

Thirteen

Mike Kanaya turned out to be a heavy-set guy in his mid-thirties, with a squarish chin, bushy eyebrows, and bright restless eyes. He was wearing a dark suit, white shirt, conservative blue-and-gray tie. He struck me as the earnest and inquisitive type, which meant, if true, that he was probably a very good newspaperman.

He was already waiting when I got to the Minami Sushi Bar in the Japan Center just before noon on Sunday. Haruko Gage must have described me to him because he popped up from his table immediately and came over and introduced himself. We shook hands, sizing each other up the way people do when they're meeting for the first time. Then we went to his corner table, and a waitress followed us over with a pot of tea and a couple of menus.

Kanaya poured tea for both of us. "Have you eaten *sushi* before?" he asked.

"No," I said. "Other kinds of Japanese food, yes, but not *sushi.*"

"You know what it is?"

"Different kinds of raw fish." And very trendy these days, among those Caucasians who like to consider themselves as being "with it." Which was why I had never tried *sushi* myself, even though Kerry had suggested it a time or two. I'm not a "with it" guy; as Leo McFate could testify, I'm just a peon.

Kanaya said, "You have no taste for raw fish?"

"I don't mind it, I guess. I kind of like *sashimi.*"

"Ah. Will you join me, then?"

"Sure," I said, because I did not want to get this meeting off to a bad start by insulting him. "Why not?"

He beckoned to the waitress and said something to her in Japanese. She went over and said something in turn to the chef behind the glass "bar" where all the *sushi* was laid out on a bed of crushed ice, and he got to work with a good deal of enthusiasm.

I decided to get down to business too. "Did Mrs. Gage tell you why I'm interested in the Yakuza?" I asked Kanaya. "The details, I mean."

"Some, but not all." He lifted his cup of tea, held it without drinking; his squarish face was serious now. "The murder of Simon Tamura, yes?"

"Yes. But I'm not investigating it; I'm trying to get disentangled from it. The Yakuza, or somebody in the Yakuza, seems to think I'm involved. A couple of men who are probably *kobun* have been following me around since I found Tamura's body. I tried talking to them a couple of times; they wouldn't talk back."

Kanaya nodded thoughtfully.

"The car they're using is registered to Ken Yamasaki," I said. "You know him?"

"Not personally. An employee of Tamura's Baths."

"Also Yakuza. And a former boyfriend of Haruko Gage."

"You don't believe Haruko is Yakuza . . . ?"

"No. Did she tell you I'm working for her?"

"Oh, yes."

"And why?"

"Yes."

"Well, there might be some connection between that and Tamura's death. If it wasn't a Yakuza killing, that is."

"Perhaps it wasn't," Kanaya said.

"Why do you say that?"

He smiled faintly. "Newspapermen have eyes and ears—and friends. The Yakuza, I am told, does not know who murdered Mr. Tamura. Or why."

So much for McFate's informant, I thought, and for McFate's theory. I said at length, "I take it Yamasaki isn't highly placed in the local chapter?"

"No. He is much too young."

"Only elders hold positions of power?"

"Except in rare cases, yes." Kanaya sipped his tea. "How much do you know of the Yakuza?"

"Not much, really. General facts, but sketchy. Very little of its background and almost nothing of how it operates."

"Few outside the Yakuza know how it operates," he said. "It is a secret and very disciplined organization, unlike any in the Western world. It pretends to believe in a code of honor and loyalty established by the sixteenth-century samurai. As proof of their loyalty, some Yakuza have cut off the first joint of the little finger and ceremoniously offered it to their *oyabun*—gang boss—in atonement for an error in judgment."

"I didn't know they could be that fanatical."

"Yes. More so than the Mafia."

"What else, Mr. Kanaya?"

"In Japan," he said, "the Yakuza controls all the major criminal activities—drugs, extortion, prostitution, gun-running, loan-sharking, pornography. But that isn't all. It also controls more than twenty-five thousand legitimate businesses, and is an important force in politics and among the corporate elite. It operates openly —far more so than any Western criminal organization. Many Yakuza offices display the gang emblem on their doors; members wear syndicate lapel pins as if they were brothers in a college fraternity." He allowed himself a small wry smile. "Believe it or not, the Yakuza even publishes its own magazine—*Yamaguchi-gumi Jiho.* Legal advice side by side with poetry and biographical features."

"Good God."

"And yet," Kanaya went on, "members of the Yakuza are self-admitted outcasts in Japanese society. Many come from the poor, undereducated classes; from Korean or Chinese minorities; even from the *burakumin*—an ancestral group ostracized for complicated reasons that involve the handling of dead animals and animal products. The word Yakuza itself . . . do you know what it means?"

"No."

"It translates as the numbers eight, nine, and three. Those numbers make up the lowest possible hand in the gambling game called *hanafuda*. A loser's hand, you see?"

I nodded. But the truth was, I saw very little. The Yakuza was a complex entity, all right; and if the Japanese themselves couldn't figure it out, or its methods, how was somebody like me supposed to? How was I supposed to get the Yakuza off my back now that it was clamped on like a damned suckerfish?

The waitress arrived with two plates and a couple of little dishes and a covered bowl of rice, set everything down in front of us, and went away again. The *sushi* looked pretty appetizing, at that. Lots of little bite-size pieces of raw fish wrapped around seasoned rice, some decorated with green stuff that was probably seaweed or yellow stuff that looked to be egg. All very attractive. My stomach started growling as I looked. The hell with attractive, it was saying, throw some of that raw fish down here and be quick about it.

I picked up my chopsticks—I'd gotten so I could use them without making a fool of myself—and poked at a piece of something on my plate. "What's this?" I asked Kanaya.

"*Hamachi*," he said. "Yellowtail."

"And this?"

"*Toro*. Tuna belly."

"Tuna . . . belly?"

"The best part of the tuna," he said. "You'll see. But first, the sauce. It's the same as for *sashimi*."

The dipping sauce was what the little dishes were for. You poured in a little soy sauce and added a blob of greenish horseradish, and the result was a moderately hot concoction that tasted pretty good. It did with *sashimi*—raw tuna—anyway. I got mine made and tried some of the yellowtail. Yeah. Not bad at all.

Kanaya started to spoon out some rice for me, but I shook my head and said, "No, I'll pass on the extra rice. I'm on a diet."

"Ah," he said.

I tasted the tuna belly. He was right: it was even better than whatever part they used for *sashimi*. When I was done chewing I said, "Tell me about the local Yakuza, Mr. Kanaya. How powerful is it, for starters?"

"In the Japanese community, quite powerful," he said. "Outside the community, not so powerful as it would like to be."

"How large is the local contingent?"

"That is difficult to estimate. There are chapters in Los Angeles and Honolulu, closely linked with the one here; members shift back and forth from one area to another. There are possibly two hundred active Yakuza on the West Coast at present, with perhaps a third in San Francisco."

"I understand Tamura was one of the local higher-ups," I said. "But he wasn't the godfather, right?"

"No. The San Francisco *oyabun* is Hisayuki Okubo."

"Does he live in the city, this Okubo?"

"Yes. On the Kara Maru."

"The restaurant ship?"

"The same."

"You mean the Yakuza runs that operation?"

"Oh, yes. A very respectable front for them."

The Kara Maru was an old Japanese freighter anchored at China Basin that had been turned into an expensive waterfront restaurant some years back. I had never been there, but it was supposed to be musty and dimly lighted and atmospheric as hell. For that reason, and because of the Bay view and because the food was said to be terrific, the tourists loved it; and so did the same "with it" crowd that frequented quaint little *sushi* bars like this one.

I said, "How accessible is Okubo?"

"Accessible?"

"Does he surround himself with bodyguards and security precautions? Or can a guy like me get in to see him without too much trouble."

"He has a bodyguards," Kanaya said. "One doesn't enter his private quarters unless invited. And he seldom leaves the Kara Maru."

"Uh-huh. I was afraid of that."

"Were you thinking of going to see him?"

"I was. I'm still considering it."

Kanaya seemed to want to say something else. Instead he picked up his bowl of rice and began to eat. I tried a piece of something that tasted like clam. Which was what it was, I found out from Kanaya. *Mirugai.* Giant clam.

I asked him some more qustions about the Yakuza, without finding out much that I didn't know or suspect already. It was reputed to have a bunch of politicians in its pocket, not all of them in Japan. It was also reputed to be making a concerted effort to dominate the lucrative Japanese tourist business in San Francisco and Los Angeles by either taking over restaurants, bars, gift shops, and entertainment facilities, or controlling them through extortion. For these reasons, it preferred to keep a low profile in this country and stay out of trouble with law enforcement agencies. Which meant, Kanaya said reassuringly, that it resorted to violence against *gaijin* only in extreme cases.

I also asked him about Simon Tamura's personal life, but there was nothing there for me either. Tamura had been a family man, had lived quietly and traditionally, hadn't gone in for the usual vices. The names Sanjiro Masaoka and Kazuo Hama meant nothing to Kanaya. Nor did he know anything about the old photograph in Tamura's office; he had never seen it.

By this time we were almost finished eating. My last piece of *sushi* was a plump gray-white thing; I hoisted it up, eyed it some more, and ate it. Not too great, but then not too bad either. Chewy. Like a chunk of fish-flavored rubber.

Kanaya asked, "Have I been of any help to you?"

"Some, yes. I appreciate your candor, Mr. Kanaya."

"It was my pleasure. Perhaps there will be a story for me to write, eventually."

"If there is," I said, "you'll be the first person I tell it to."

"Ah."

"Meanwhile, lunch is on me."

He made a slight bow with his head. *"Arigato gozaimas'.* You enjoyed the *sushi,* then?"

"It was fine. Except for that last piece. Grayish thing, sort of chewy?"

"Tako," he said. "Octopus."

I was sorry I'd asked.

* * * *

When I got outside, the rain and the white Ford were both there waiting for me—another pair of joyless certainties, like death and taxes, that I seemed to be cursed with these days. One of the *kobun*, the putty-nosed guy, had followed me inside the Japan Center and hung around out in the mall somewhere while I had my meeting with Mike Kanaya; he was behind me again now, and when I crossed to where my car was parked on Post Street he went and rejoined his friend in the Ford, half a block away.

I was still fed up with having them around all the time, but what Kanaya had told me about Yakuza policy toward non-Japanese had taken some of the edge off my anxiety. And the thought of the two of them sitting a cold, cramped watch all night in the rain, as they had probably done, made me feel there might be some justice in this world after all.

The rain slackened to a fine mist as I drove back up the hill to Pacific Heights. I took the only legal parking space on my block, so that the Ford had to pull over and stop in somebody's driveway. They were still parked there, watching, as I entered my building.

I had tried calling the Hama Egg Ranch again this morning, just before I left for Japantown, and that time I'd got a busy signal; so somebody was home up there today. I intended to give it one more shot, and if I still couldn't get through, then maybe it was time to pay my first and no doubt last visit to the Kara Maru restaurant. Maybe I couldn't beard Hisayuki Okubo without an invitation, but there was no harm in trying. I hoped.

So I dialed the 707 area code for Petaluma, then the Hama number, and the thing rang six times before I finally heard an answering click, just as I was getting ready to hang up. A woman's voice, hoarse and a little on the quavery side, said, "Hello? Yes, please?"

I gave my name and where I was calling from. Then I said, "I'd like to speak to Mr. Hama, Mr. Kazuo Hama."

Silence.

"Ma'am? Hello?"

"No," she said. "No, no."

"You mean Mr. Hama isn't there?"

"Not here," she said, "Kazuo is *dead!*" and I heard her begin to weep just before she broke the connection.

Fourteen

I got up to Petaluma a little before three-thirty. The rain didn't follow me all the way; it quit just north of San Rafael, and there were thin blue veins in the cloud pattern when I took the first Petaluma exit off Highway 101.

The white Ford didn't follow me at all. But that was my choice, not theirs. When I'd left my flat I had driven down to Fisherman's Wharf, where the traffic is always congested and the tourists are out even in wet weather, and did some tricky maneuvers involving other cars and stop signals; the last I'd seen of the Ford had been at an intersection near The Cannery, tangled up behind a smoke-belching Muni bus. It's not all that difficult to shake a tail if you set your mind to it and expend some effort. And I just did not feel like going all the way to Petaluma with those two dragging after me like a couple of loose anchors.

The main street used to be called that, Main Street. Now it was called Petaluma Boulevard South and Petaluma Boulevard North, with the dividing line being the middle of town. The place used to be a small agricultural community with a population of around ten thousand, built mostly on the west side of Petaluma Creek—a narrow salt-water estuary that wound down through fourteen miles of tule marshes to San Pablo Bay. Now it was a place where San Francisco office workers lived and commuted from, a bedroom community with a population of over forty thousand, most of whom lived on the east side of the Petaluma River—creek becoming river by act of the state legislature. Once it had been famous as "The Egg Basket of the World" because it was the world's leading producer of chickens and chicken fruit in the early years of the century, shipping millions of eggs annually from dozens of surrounding ranches. Now it was famous as the "Hell no, we won't grow" city, the place that in 1972 had passed a limited-growth ordinance hailed by environmentalists and traditionalists, fought bitterly by developers who had gobbled up most of the land in and out of the city limits. In the old days, riverboats and barges and cargo schooners used to make regular runs up and down the creek, carrying hay, alfalfa, eggs, livestock, and passengers. In the new days, speedboats and small yachts traveled the river and tied up in the basin behind the old brick complex of restaurants and shops that had once been a feed mill.

Progress. Changing times. Some liked the idea, some didn't. I didn't, but then I had no stake in the town's past or in its future. Why should I cry for Petaluma? Petaluma wasn't going to cry for me.

I stopped at a service station and got directions to Rainsville Road. Following them, I drove out Petaluma Boulevard North to Stony Point Road, turned west on Stony Point, and came to Rainsville after less than half a mile. Another half-mile brought me to a rain-puddled gravel driveway and a sign that said: HAMA EGG RANCH. Below that, in smaller letters, were the words: ONE OF PETALUMA'S LARGEST. And in still smaller letters: EGGS, FRYERS, ROASTING HENS • BABY CHICKS FOR SALE.

One of Petaluma's largest, I thought as I swung into the driveway. But that didn't mean much these days. The egg industry up here was only a gaunt shadow of what it once had been. One conglomerate outfit owned most of the ranches; there were only a few independents like Hama left. And all the hatcheries and feed companies that had once flourished were long gone. Now Kazuo Hama was gone too. How? And why?

The drive was lined on one side by eucalyptus trees planted as windbreaks. The ranch began its outward sprawl just beyond the trees—a familiar layout that gave me a vague, fleeting nostalgia because I had worked on a chicken ranch one summer in my teens, so long ago that the memory of it was faded and distorted, like a very old daguerrotype. The nearest buildings were a large white clapboard house, a tankhouse, and a garage with a wing tacked onto it that was probably a workshop. Opposite and beyond that little cluster was a small barnlike structure that was probably the grainery, where feed and supplies were kept and eggs were packed for shipment. The chicken houses came next, half a dozen of them, each one seventy-

five-feet long—large enough for maybe a thousand laying hens—
made of wood and built up off the ground, with a V-shaped roof and
screened windows to let in light. Fenced-in yards stretched out
alongside each of the houses, and in them hundreds of white leg-
horns pranced and pecked and drank from rain-swollen troughs.

There were two cars drawn up in a little parking area near the
fenced yard of the ranchhouse—a newish Isuzu and a mud-caked
pickup truck. I parked next to the pickup. From over in the chicken
yards I could hear a constant fluttering of wings, with cackling noises
mingled in. But I didn't look over there; I did not want to think
about chickens any more. Or about eggs. They reminded me of my
diet, and made me hungry again in spite of myself.

I walked over to the front gate and along a crushed-shell path
and up the stairs to the porch. I wasn't trying to be quiet about it,
but I must have managed just the same because the two people
talking inside the house didn't break off their conversation. I could
hear them plainly; there was a closed screen door, but the front
door behind it was standing open, evidently to allow fresh air to
circulate. Their words sounded interesting. So instead of knocking
right away, I stood there and listened. Occupational license. Private eyes were supposed to be keyhole snoopers and eavesdroppers,
after all.

". . . don't understand this at all, Johnny," a woman's voice was
saying. It wasn't the same woman I'd talked to on the phone; this
one was much younger. "A *mausoleum,* and all those years of upkeep. Why would he have done a thing like that?"

"I don't know," a man's voice said. Also young, also unfamiliar.
"How should I know?"

"Well, there aren't any Wakasas around here."

"Not now. Maybe there were after the war."

"Are you *sure* you don't know who that woman was?"

"How many times do I have to tell you?"

"I thought Father might have confided in you . . ."

"Man-talk, eh? You think he had an affair with this Chiyoko
Wakasa, don't you?"

"Sshh! Do you want Mother to hear?"

I was listening good now. Chiyoko—Haruko's middle name, and

the name that had been written on the package containing the medallion.

"Well?" the man's voice said, a little more quietly. "That's what you think, isn't it?"

"It's what *you* think too."

"How do you know what I think? I don't think anything. Maybe she was an old relative of the family or something."

"You know we don't have any relatives named Wakasa."

"It could have been her married name . . ."

"Oh God, Johnny, she wasn't a relative and you know it!"

"What difference does it make who she was? She's been dead almost forty years. And now he's dead too. What does it *matter* anymore?"

"It matters," the woman said stubbornly. "Are we supposed to keep on paying the upkeep on this . . . this stranger's burial place?"

"It's only a few dollars a year. Father kept paying it; it must have been important to him. We should pay it in honor of his memory."

"I still want to know who she was. A mausoleum at Cypress Hill! Of all things!"

"Come on, it's not that strange."

"Isn't it? Did you ever hear of anything like that around here?"

"Plenty of Japanese are Catholics . . ."

"But *we're* not. I just don't understand it."

"Janet," the man said in exasperated tones, "you worry too much about little things. Worry about the big things for a change, like these files and papers. I don't want to spend all night sorting them out."

A couple of seconds of silence. Then, "I guess you're right. Do you want to see if Mother needs anything before we get back to it? Some more tea?"

"Yes, okay."

The sound of footsteps, fading. Then silence. I shuffled my feet, making some noise, and reached out and knocked on the screen door's wooden frame.

The woman came after a few seconds and peered out at me, then drew the door open. She was thirtyish, slender, very attractive, with her black hair tied up tight on her head; wearing a black skirt and a black sweater—mourning clothes. "Oh, hello," she said solemnly.

Then she said, "I'm afraid we're closed, if you want to buy something. There's been a death in the family."

I feigned surprise. "I'm very sorry to hear that. I hope it wasn't
Mr. Kazuo Hama."

"Yes, it was. Did you come to see my father?"

"On a personal matter, yes. May I ask when he passed away?"

"Four days ago. His funeral was yesterday."

"A sudden illness?"

"No. He . . . he was killed. A hit-and-run accident."

"Have the police found the person responsible?"

"Not yet."

"Where did it happen?"

"On the road out front. He'd gone to get the mail."

"Then there were no witnesses?"

"No. None."

"Did your father wear a white jade ring, by any chance?"

"Yes, but it's missing—" She broke off and frowned at me. "You
said you came to see him on a personal matter?"

"That's right, Miss . . . ?"

"Mrs. Janet Ito. And *your* name, please?"

I made one up—Allan Barker—and made up a profession to go
with it. I didn't like the idea of lying to her, lying in the face of grief,
but it was easier and kinder and more prudent than telling her the
truth; the truth would only have led to questions and stirred up a
lot of ugly suspicion. "I'm a lawyer," I said, "representing the estate
of Mr. Simon Tamura in San Francisco."

The Tamura name didn't seem to mean anything to her. She said,
"Yes?" blankly.

"Mr. Tamura and your father were old friends, you know."

"No, I didn't know."

"He never spoke of Mr. Tamura?"

"Not that I can recall."

"But surely he mentioned Sanjiro Masaoka?"

She frowned again. "I don't know that name either."

"Well, that's odd," I said. "Mr. Tamura kept an old photograph
of the three of them on the wall of his office. He said they were very
good friends as youths back in the forties."

"Oh," she said, "the camp, maybe."

"Camp?"

"The Tule Lake camp." Her mouth wrinkled up as if the words tasted bitter."The Tule Lake *concentration* camp. My father was incarcerated there during the war."

"Oh, I see."

"For four years. He was a Nisei, as patriotic as any native with white skin. It was a terrible ordeal for him; he never really got over it."

"I'm sorry about that too, Mrs. Ito."

She nodded as if she thought my response was a proper one. Not just from me; from all Caucasians of my generation, all the war hysterics in California and Washington who had been responsible for the displacement of more than a hundred thousand Japanese-Americans, for forcing them to sell or abandon their land and their belongings and then hauling them off to "relocation centers" like the one at Tule Lake, up in the northeast section of the state. And when Issei and Nisei were let out after the war, and allowed to return to what was left of their homes, there had been no reparation, no attempt at all to rectify any of the damage that had been done. Janet Ito had every right to be bitter about that shameful little episode in American history, even though she herself hadn't been born at the time.

I said, "Was your mother also interned at the Tule Lake camp?"

"No. She was at Minidoka in Idaho. She met my father here in Petaluma just after the war."

"Could you give me the names of one or two of your father's friends who were also at Tule Lake?"

The frown reappeared. "Why are you asking all these questions?" she said. "Just what did you want to see my father about, anyway?"

I had an answer ready, not a very good one, but I didn't get to use it. There was the sound of footsteps again and a man materialized through a doorway behind Janet Ito. He gave me a curious look, hesitated, and then moved up to stand behind her left shoulder. He was about her age, maybe a couple of years younger, and you could see a marked resemblence between them. Same facial contours, same slenderness, same sort of quiet good looks.

"Is Mother all right?" Janet Ito asked him. But her eyes were still on me.

"Yes."

He didn't ask who I was, but it was plain that he wanted to know. She sensed it, too. She said, "This is Mr. Barker, Johnny. A lawyer from San Francisco. He says he came to see Father on a personal matter of some sort."

He winced. "You tell him what happened?"

"She told me," I said. "Are you Mrs. Ito's brother?"

"That's right. John Hama."

"I'm sorry about your father, Mr. Hama." He nodded, and I went on, "The reason I'm here is that I'm trying to locate a young woman named Haruko Gage. That's her married name, Gage; her maiden name was Fujita. A man named Simon Tamura died in San Francisco recently and left Mrs. Gage a substantial amount of money. I represent the Tamura estate, you see, and we're having difficulty determining Mrs. Gage's present whereabouts."

Blank, steady looks from both of them. John Hama said, "What does that have to do with us?"

I gave him the same explanation I'd given his sister, saying that I'd hoped their father could offer me a lead to Haruko Gage. More lies; I did not care for myself too much just then. And like most lies, they got me nowhere. John Hama seemed never to have heard of Simon Tamura, Sanjiro Masaoka, or Haruko Gage nee Fujita. There were Fujitas living in the Petaluma area, he said, but he knew the families and none of the women was called Haruko. He did agree with his sister that Kazu Hama could have known Tamura and Masaoka at the Tule Lake camp. His father had almost never spoken of that period in his life.

I tried the question on him that Janet Ito had refused to answer: "Could you tell me the names of one or two of your father's friends who were also at Tule Lake?"

He was not nearly as suspicious as she was. He said promptly, "Well, there's old Charley Takeuchi. He and my father were working as chicken sexers for the Pioneer Hatchery when the war came; they went to Tule Lake together."

Chicken-sexing, I knew from my teen-age summer on the egg ranch, was a process whereby day-old chicks were examined to determine if they were roosters or pullets. The process had been invented by a Japanese and most chicken sexers, for whatever reason, were of that race.

"Where would I find Mr. Takeuchi?" I asked.

"Well, he's retired now and lives in town with his sister. On Bassett Street, near the high school—number three-twenty-nine."

"Is there anyone else you can think of?"

He lifted one shoulder and let it drop. "Janet? Can you think of anybody else?"

"No," she said. The frown and the suspicion were still on her face, and I thought that she was getting ready to ask me how talking to Charley Takeuchi about the Tule Lake camp was going to help me find Haruko Gage. I had no answer for that; or for questions about how I'd known her father had worn a white jade ring. And if she decided to ask for identification, which she probably would, I had none that said I was a lawyer named Allan Barker. I had found out all I could reasonably expect to; it was time for me to leave before trouble developed that all three of us didn't need.

I said, "Well. Thank you for talking to me. And I'm sorry again about your father; I know this must be a difficult time for you."

"It's never easy when somebody you love dies," John Hama said.

That made me feel even worse. And yet, I told myself as I went down the steps and over to my car, the eavesdropping and the deception were excusable if they helped find out who had run down and killed Kazuo Hama. Sure they were. Unless the finding and its aftermath dragged some sort of ugliness in Hama's past out into the open so his family would have to cope with it—ugliness that maybe involved a woman named Chiyoko Wakasa and a mausoleum in Cypress Hill Cemetery. Would it all be worth it then, the lies that led to the truth, the big hunt for justice?

Questions like that were unsettling; I couldn't deal with them, not now. I wasn't a metaphysician, I was a detective. Detectives dealt in facts, not abstracts. Detectives *had* to believe in the big hunt for justice, because if they didn't, what was the purpose of their existence? If truth and justice had no fundamental meaning, then their lives had none either.

I got into the car and started the engine. When I glanced up at the house John Hama was gone but Janet Ito was still standing in the open doorway, looking after me. I backed the car up and took myself out of her life, at least for the time being.

All right: facts. Simon Tamura, Kazuo Hama, and Sanjiro Masaoka had all been killed within a few days of each other, under questionable circumstances at best. A medallion that might have belonged to Tamura and a locket that might have belonged to Masaoka had been sent to Haruko Gage anonymously; something that might have belonged to Hama—the white jade ring—had also been presented to her. Why? What was the common denominator between Haruko and three dead men in their sixties, whom she claimed not to know, and who may or may not have known each other at the Tule Lake Relocation Center in the early 1940s?

More facts: The name Chiyoku, Haruko's middle name, had been written on the last package. Kazuo Hama had buried one Chiyoku Wakasa sometime after the end of World War II. What was the connection there? *Was* there one? And if there was, who was Chiyoku Wakasa? And how and why had she died? And why had Hama erected a mausoleum for her remains?

Lots of facts now, lots of bright slippery mismatched beads waiting to be strung together. Yet the more of them I gathered, the more puzzling and complex the whole business became. It seemed I was no closer to grasping the truth now than I had been when I'd started.

The long shadows of dusk were gathering; I switched on my headlights as I drove back toward Petaluma. The beams reflected off rainwater in a flooded culvert ahead and gave it, for just a second or two, the look of shimmering quicksilver.

Fifteen

Cypress Hill Cemetery fronted on Magnolia Avenue, a few blocks off Petaluma Boulevard on the northern outskirts of town. Another stop at a service station got me that information; it also got me directions to Bassett Street, where Charley Takeuchi lived. But the cemetery was closer and on the way, and the time was almost five o'clock, so I headed there first.

There were two cemeteries, actually, a newish-looking one and then an older and more interesting one, both built on small wooded hillsides and both surrounded by low cyclone fences. The older one was Cypress Hill. Just inside the entrance drive were stone caretakers' buildings, and a sloping green lawn opposite with neat little gravestones laid flat to mark the graves that dotted it—a current burial fashion, apparently devised to make a cemetery look like a visually ascetic garden instead. Either that, or to make it easier to mow the grass. Up beyond the lawn was an older section where tombstones and monuments jutted up among the shadows of cypress, palms, live oaks. In the gray-purple twilight I could also make out the blocky shapes of at least three small mausoleums.

It was just five o'clock when I turned in at the entrance. One half of the gate barred the way across the drive and there was an old green Plymouth parked in front of it. An elderly guy in a raincoat and hat was getting ready to close the other gate-half, but he stopped when my headlights picked him up. He stood there with a padlock in one hand, squinting in my direction.

I set the brake and got out without shutting off the engine. When I came up to him he said, "Sorry, neighbor. Closing up now; you'll have to come back tomorrow."

"I won't be here tomorrow," I said. "I'm a stranger in town."

"Too bad," he said, but not as if he meant it.

"I only need five to ten minutes. I want to take a look at one of the mausoleums."

"Can't spare the time. Another night, maybe, but I got to be out to Penngrove by five-thirty. Lodge doings."

"Well, maybe you can tell me what I need to know. That is, if you're the regular caretaker here."

"Now who else would I be? A graverobber?" He thought that was funny and laughed to prove it. "A graverobber," he said, and waited like a stand-up comic for his laugh.

I obliged him, just to keep him friendly. "I'm trying to find out about a woman named Chiyoko Wakasa—"

"Who?"

"Chiyoko Wakasa. One of the mausoleums is hers."

"Oh, yeah, the Jap woman. Can't tell you nothing about her, neighbor. She was before my time."

"You remember the date of her death, offhand?"

"No. Look, I got to take off now. Else I won't make Penngrove by five-thirty."

Now that I was here, I was reluctant to leave empty-handed. So I said, "How would it be if you went to Penngrove and I went in and took a look at the Wakasa mausoleum? I won't be more than a few minutes and I'll padlock the gate for you when I go."

He shook his head. "Can't do that, neighbor. Against the rules. Besides, I don't know you."

"What do I look like?" I said. "A graverobber?"

I laughed and he laughed with me. Then his expression got crafty; and that was good, because it meant he was going to be the one to bring up money. "Well now," he said, "if it's that important to you, and if you was to show me some identification, and if you was to maybe pay me a little something to ease my conscience, I guess maybe I could allow it."

"How does five dollars sound?"

"Five dollars always sounds good, neighbor. But ten dollars sounds even better."

"Then again," I said, "Five dollars sounds a lot better than nothing at all."

We grinned at each other like a couple of sly vultures. And I got my wallet out and showed him my driver's license and then watched him produce a scrap of paper from his pocket and write down my name and the license number of my car. After which I gave him the five dollars, and he said, "A pleasant evening to you, neighbor," and handed me the padlock.

He didn't leave right away; he waited until I drove inside, got out again, and shut the other half of the gate. Then he was satisfied. The Plymouth disappeared, and I headed up the cypress-lined drive toward the cemetery's older section.

Up there, the graves were laid out in big squarish plots with raised cement borders, some family and some communal, like lots in a miniature housing development. Narrow roadways and narrower paths, all rough and unpaved and strewn with storm residue, made a kind of irregular grid pattern over the grounds. It was pretty dark now, and there wasn't any form of night-lighting; but the mausoleums were still visibly outlined against the restless sky. I turned toward the nearest one. My headlamps splashed wobbles of light over the dark looming shapes of the trees, over tall marble obelisks and squat stone monuments and ancient wooden markers like bleached bones imbedded in the earth.

When I came abreast of the first mausoleum I unclipped the flashlight I keep under the dash and went to look at the inscription over the door. Not the right one. I got a bearing on a second mausoleum, higher up and back toward the rear perimeter fence, and moved behind the wheel again and drove up there.

This was the oldest part of Cypress Hill, judging from the condition of the plots and the look of the tombstones. The grave next to the mausoleum had buckled and collapsed in the middle from the encroachment of tree roots; moss grew thickly in the chips and cracks of the cement. The headlights were aimed at the stone marker when I braked to a stop, and I could read part of its date: DIED 1875. AGED 44 YEARS, 9 MONTHS.

The burial vault itself bulked up in the shadows of a pair of live oaks. It was about the size of a large shed, made out of cut-stone blocks, its entrance flanked by two Corinthian columns and two sculpted stone urns overflowing with moss. It looked as though it had been there for a good many years. I took it to be the final resting place of one of Petaluma's pioneering families—the town had been founded back in the 1850s, on land that had once belonged to the Mexican general Vallejo—but I got out with the flashlight to make sure.

And it turned out I was wrong. This was the mausoleum I was looking for, the one Kazuo Hama had built not so long ago. Words and dates cut into the stone above the entrance read:

CHIYOKO WAKASA
1924—1947
"THERE THE WICKED CEASE FROM TROUBLING,
AND THE WEARY BE AT REST"

I stood for a time, holding the flash beam on the inscription. She'd been twenty-three years old when she died. Twenty-three was too young for death; she had hardly even lived. Who was she? What had happened to her?

"There the wicked cease from troubling, and the weary be at rest." I wasn't familiar with the quotation, though it was probably Biblical. An odd sort of inscription for one Japanese-American to put on the tomb of another—almost as odd as erecting the mausoleum itself. Did it imply that Chiyoko Wakasa had been wicked and weary both, at the age of twenty-three?

I made a circuit of the building, to see if there were any other markings. There weren't. A stained-glass window had been set into the rear wall—a religious cross in yellow and red, indicating that Chiyoko Wakasa had been a Catholic—but that was all I found. Back at the entrance again, I paused and played my flash over the decorative iron gate that barred the door. Then, without any conscious purpose, the way you do things sometimes, I reached out and tugged at one of the bars.

The latch made a clicking noise and the gate popped open in my hand.

I hadn't been aware of the wind before, but now I felt it like a cold caress on the back of my neck. There were marks, scratches, on the gate's side; I could see them in the torchlight. Not brand-new scratches, but not old ones either. I moved the flash over to the latch plate set into the wall. Marks there, too, gouges in the metal and chips in the stone. The gate had been forced open with some kind of tool, probably a crowbar, and then reclosed so the caretakers and groundsmen wouldn't notice the tampering.

Kazuo Hama wouldn't have done it, I thought. There would not have been any need; he'd built the mausoleum and that meant he'd had a key, or at least access to a key. The person who'd killed Hama and the others, then? But why? Why break into a mausoleum?

The door was made out of some kind of heavy wood bound with iron strips. I switched the flash to my left hand and reached down and caught hold of the handle. Nothing happened when I pulled on it. But when I shoved against the door, it creaked open like the one on the old "Inner Sanctum" radio program.

I smelled the flowers immediately, even before I saw them in the flash beam. The fragrance seemed to rush out at me like something sentient that had been trapped in there—a musty-sweet, cloying fragrance, intensified by the cold night air, that made you think of death and slow decay. Then the light picked up the flowers, and it was like looking into a dark room in a funeral parlor, the room where they lay a body out in its coffin so mourners can look at it.

Roses, mostly—yellow and pink, red and white. Cut roses in cans of water, some fresh and some dry and blackened and rotting. Small rose bushes in planter tubs. Carnations, gladiola, lilies, two or three other varieties I couldn't identify. Covering most of the floor space in there, leaning against the walls, draped over the stone bier set under the stained-glass window.

Smelling the flowers, seeing them in there by torchlight, made my hackles rise. It was eerie; and it smacked of aberration and madness. No sane mind could have broken into the mausoleum of a woman dead for thirty-six years and filled it with all those floral tributes.

I moved inside, using the light to guide my way so I wouldn't trip over any of the cans or tubs. When I got to the bier I circled it, playing the flash over its surfaces, looking for any signs of tampering there. But the burial crypt was still sealed. The person responsible for the flowers was not a ghoul, at least.

There wasn't anything else to see in the narrow confines of the vault. And the musty-sweet odor was starting to make me queasy. I followed the light out into the cold, fresh air, shut it off, and then pulled the door shut. I was reaching for the gate when I heard the noise.

It wasn't much of a noise—a crackling, sliding sound that came from some distance away, but clear in the night-hush that lay over the cemetery. Still, as I swung around toward it, the hackles went up again on my neck. It had come from beyond my car, where the hillside leveled off and there were no more graves, just trees and underbrush lining the perimeter fence. But all I could see up there were thick shadows: tree branches swaying in the wind, nothing that seemed to be moving at ground level.

An animal, I thought. A raccoon or a skunk or something. I let out the breath I'd been holding, took a step toward the car.

The crackling and scraping came again, and this time I saw something move that wasn't a tree branch—something big, a man-shaped shadow that detached itself from the other shadows for an instant before blending back into them.

Impulsively, I ran over to the car, around behind it so I wouldn't be illuminated in the headlight glare, and then up a soggy path past a couple of oaks and the last of the crumbling old graves. I could see the fence, then, and more movement on the other side of it, somebody running away into a thick stand of eucalyptus. I kept on going across open ground, through wet grass and rotting humus, switching the flash back on as I ran; but the beam wasn't powerful enough to penetrate the darkness more than thirty yards ahead, and the running figure was a good fifty yards away from me now.

At the fence I hesitated, thought about climbing over and continuing the chase, and decided it was a foolish idea. I didn't know those woods; I could blunder around in them and get myself lost. Or ambushed, for that matter. Besides, it didn't have to have been Chiyoko Wakasa's belated mourner. It could have been a tramp. Or a kid; kids were always hanging around cemeteries, looking for mischief.

It wasn't a tramp or a kid, I thought.

I turned around and started back toward the path. And behind me, then, a long way off, I heard a car engine start up and then the faint shriek of rubber on pavement.

No, it hadn't been a tramp or a kid at all.

Sixteen

Three-twenty-nine Bassett Street was maybe ten blocks from downtown, three blocks from City Hall and the police station, and half a block from Petaluma High School. The house itself was an old frame job, painted white, with a glassed-in porch to the right of an old-fashioned walled staircase. Lights burned on the porch, and rattan blinds were only partially drawn over the windows; when I went up the stairs I could see a short, thin, wispy-haired old man sitting in there with his feet on a hassock, watching a television program.

I could still see him as I pushed the doorbell. He sat up, swiveled his head around, blinked at me from behind thick glasses, then got to his feet and blinked at me again and disappeared. Ten seconds later the door opened on a chain and he looked out at me warily. He appeared to be between seventy and eighty; his face was as wrinkled as a raisin. He didn't say anything.

"Mr. Takeuchi? Charley Takeuchi?"

"I don't know you," he said.

"No, sir, you don't. John Hama gave me your name and address."

His expression softened a little; the grief that came into his eyes gave them a liquidy look, like chocolate pudding. "You know his father was killed?"

"Yes. That's part of the reason I'm here."

"Kazuo and I were friends forty-five years. That's a long time."

"Yes, it is. I'm sorry, Mr. Takeuchi."

"*Shikata ga nai,*" he said. "Did you know Kazuo?"

"I'm afraid we never met."

"A good man. A good friend." His eyes fluttered behind his glasses. "What is it you want with me?"

"To ask you about some people Mr. Hama used to know. Friends of his back in the forties."

"The forties," Mr. Takeuchi said. "The war. That was a bad time."

"Wars are always bad times."

"But that one, that war . . ." He shook his head.

"The two men are Simon Tamura and Sanjiro Masaoka."

He repeated the names, slowly. Then he nodded and made a wry mouth and said, "Oh, those two. They weren't Kazuo's friends. He thought they were, but they weren't. They only got him in trouble."

"What sort of trouble?"

"Trouble," he said, and shrugged.

"When was this? During the war?"

"Yes, the war."

"At the Tule Lake camp?"

His mouth pinched up; the look that crossed his expressive face this time was one of pain. "That place," he said. "*Makura moto!*"

"I don't understand, Mr. Takeuchi."

"A terrible place to sleep. To live."

"And that was where Simon Tamura and Sanjiro Masaoka got Mr. Hama in trouble?"

"It was. Stealing, making insults, blowing bugles before dawn. Other things."

"What other things?"

"I don't know. I never wanted to know."

"Mr. Hama didn't speak about them?"

"Not about them, not about that place. He was a good boy after the war; he worked hard with his chickens. I worked hard too. And now I'm old and I have no money and my sister takes care of me." He shrugged again.

"Did Mr. Hama have a girlfriend at Tule Lake?"

"Girlfriend? No, I don't think so."

"Did he know a woman there named Chiyoko Wakasa?"

Mr. Takeuchi was silent for ten seconds or so; he seemed to be searching his memory. "I don't remember," he said finally. "I don't believe I ever knew a woman called Chiyoko."

"She was about Mr. Hama's age. She died in 1947, here in Petaluma or somewhere nearby."

"There was a Wakasa family here once. Yes, Michio Wakasa— a gardener. But they moved away."

"Did Michio Wakasa have a daughter?"

"I don't remember."

"When did the family move away?"

"A long time ago."

"Could it have been in the late forties?"

"It could have been."

"Do you know where they moved to?"

"No," he said. "No."

"Did you and Mr. Hama talk much recently?"

The question seemed to confuse him. "Recently?"

"Before he died. The past few weeks."

"Sometimes we talked. He came to visit sometimes."

"Did he ever mention a woman named Haruko Gage? Or Haruko Fujita?"

"All these names, all these questions," he said. The confusion was still in his eyes. "Why do you want to know so many things?"

For the second time that day I lied into the face of grief—the same lies I had told Janet Ito and John Hama. And this time, they got me nothing at all. They didn't even get me invited inside Charley Takeuchi's house, where I might have been able to chip a little more out of his memory; instead, they had the opposite effect.

"Lawyers," he said, and made the wry mouth again. "I don't like lawyers. I had trouble with lawyers once, when my wife died. Questions, questions, and then legal tricks and all my money was gone."

"I'm not that kind of lawyer, Mr. Takeuchi—"

"That's what *they* said. You leave now. My sister will be home soon; I have to help her cook dinner."

And he shut the door gently, almost politely. A moment later I heard the snicking sound of a dead-bolt being thrown inside.

I went back down to the car. I would have liked to look through the back files of Petaluma's newspaper—the *Argus-Courier;* I'd seen the building on Petaluma Boulevard North—for some mention of how Chiyoko Wakasa had died in 1947. I would also have liked to make the rounds of Japanese families in the area until I located somebody who had either known Chiyoko Wakasa or who had been at the Tule Lake camp during the war and could tell me more about the Tamura-Hama-Masaoka triumvirate. But I couldn't reasonably do either of those things tonight, and I had no desire to stay over because there were also things I wanted to do in San Francisco. Like getting Haruko to give me the white jade ring, the gold locket, and the medallion, then turning them over to the police and pleading with either Jack Logan or McFate to run a check on the items that would verify their origins. And like finding out more background on the Tule Lake Relocation Center, from a man who ought to know and who I'd been planning to talk to again anyway: Nelson Mixer.

But the main reason I was heading back was Haruko herself. I was more convinced than ever, after what the Hama family had told me and what I'd seen tonight at Cypress Hill Cemetery, that her unknown admirer was a homicidal psychopath. He hadn't done anything to Haruko except shower her with presents taken off men he'd murdered, but the line between love and hate was a fine one in the sanest of individuals; in the mind of a psycho, it was almost invisible. I was going to have to tell her that, like it or not, because I wanted her and Artie to go away somewhere for a while, out of harm's way. Just in case.

*   *   *   *

As soon as I got home I checked the answering machine—one message, Kerry saying she felt better and would I call her—and then dialed the Gage number. No answer. Out somewhere, dinner or something; it was a quarter of eight. But I could feel a vague uneasiness stirring around inside my head.

Instead of calling Kerry right away, I headed into the kitchen. Food before love, food to soothe the nerves: I was famished. The only things in the refrigerator were eggs and carrots and the container of pineapple yogurt and a package of gray-looking ground sirloin that had been there a while. I sniffed the meat. It didn't smell too bad; and there weren't any funny little white things crawling around in it. So I broiled it in the oven, soft-boiled three eggs, and ate two carrots and the yogurt while I waited. None of it tasted very good, but it did combine to fill the rumbling hole under my breastbone.

Back in the bedroom, I looked up Wakasa in the San Francisco telephone directory. No listing for anyone by that name. I would have to call Harry Fletcher at the DMV again tomorrow, I thought. Even if Michio Wakasa was no longer alive, there might be suriving members of his family still living in California—somebody, maybe, who had known the woman Chiyoku and who could answer my questions about her.

I tried the Gage number again. Still no answer.

So I called Kerry and talked to her a while. I told her about my trip to Petaluma and I told her about the two *kobun;* I didn't tell her the Yakuza had been following her around too, because I didn't want to upset her. We both would have liked me to go over and spend the night at her place, but it was late and we both had to be up early in the morning. And tomorrow night was out because she had a business dinner with her boss and an agency client. So we had to settle for Tuesday night at my place; her neighbors were fighting again, which usually meant constant yelling and things being broken against walls.

Still nobody home at the Gage house.

I rang up Eberhardt. It took him six rings to answers, and when he did he sounded sleepy and disgruntled. "I feel asleep," he said. "I was watching this movie, *The Horse Soldiers,* pretty good old Western with John Wayne, and I just corked off. Christ, I must be getting old."

"I know the feeling."

"Maybe I ought to stock up on some Geritol. So what've you been up to since Friday? The Yakuza still bothering you?"

"Still following me around, yeah. But it's not the Yakuza I'm worried about right now." And I told him what I'd been up to since Friday, what I *was* worried about.

He didn't say much until I was finished. "Sounds like you might be onto something pretty hairy, all right," he said then. "But where's your proof all three of those Japanese guys were killed by the same person? Where's the motive? Hell, you can't even prove murder in two of the deaths."

"I know it," I said. "But I can't just sit on it, Eb. What if this loony decides to go after Haruko Gage next?"

"Talk to her. Tell her to take a little vacation."

"I intend to. But she can't stay on vacation indefinitely."

"You got some leads to follow up. Maybe you can prove a connection between the Tamura homicide and the Gage woman."

"I've got a connection, remember? The medallion. And that white jade ring links her to Kazuo Hama's death. And the gold locket links her to Sanjiro Masaoka's death."

"So you say. But all McFate and the local boys are interested in is the Tamura case—unless you can show 'em hard evidence that it's linked to the other two. Which means *you* got to establish those pieces of jewelry belonged to the three dead guys."

"I thought maybe Jack Logan would listen to reason."

"I doubt it. He goes by the book, the same as McFate. The same as I used to, for that matter. But I'll tell you what: I'll go talk to Jack myself in the morning, lay it out for him. He's more liable to listen to me anyhow; and if he buys it, you can take it from there. Sound okay?"

"Sounds fine. Thanks, Eb."

"*De nada.*"

He asked me for the details again—names, dates—and wrote them down as I talked. I was feeling pretty kindly toward him just then. Maybe it wasn't going to be so bad having Eberhardt for a partner after all. In fact, maybe it was going to be damned good having him around.

When I was done filling him in he said, "Check with me at the office after ten sometime; that's when the telephone company guy's coming in to install the phones. If you can't get there for any reason, why don't you call that custom-shirt outfit on the floor below? Slim-Taper Shirts, I think the name is. I'll stop by there in the morning and ask them to send somebody up to get me if you call."

"Good idea."

"What color phone you want, by the way?"

"Any color," I said, "except pimp yellow."

Another call to the Gage house. Another dozen rings without a response. I was starting to get worried now, even though it was still relatively early—not yet ten o'clock.

I went and ran some bathwater and got into the tub with a 1948 issue of *New Detective*. There were some good writers in that issue —John D. MacDonald, William Campbell Gault—but I was too tense to stay with any of the stories. I gave it up at a quarter to eleven, dried off, put on my old chenille robe, and headed for the phone again.

And this time, on the fourth ring, there was an answering click and I heard Haruko Gage's voice.

I let out a breath and told her who was calling, resisting an impulse to ask her where the hell she'd been; it was none of my business, really, now that I knew she was safe. Then I asked her if the name Chiyoko Wakasa meant anything to her, and she said no, she didn't know anyone named Wakasa. She sounded honestly puzzled.

"Do you know anybody who was at the Tule Lake Relocation Center during World War II?" I asked.

"No . . . well, yes, one or two people, I guess. Mr. Tamura was; Ken Yamasaki told me that. What does Tule Lake have to do with anything? And who is Chiyoko Wakasa?"

"I wish I knew. What I do know is too complicated to go into on the phone; suppose we let it wait until morning. I can come by your place around nine . . ."

"I have a business appointment at nine, downtown. With a representative of one of the companies Art and I design for. I could probably break it at the last minute, but . . ."

"How long do you expect it'll last?"

"Until noon or so. I should be back here no later than one o'clock."

"How about if I meet you at your place at one?"

"All right. Are you sure . . . I mean, there's nothing I ought to know right away, is there?"

"No. Don't worry, Mrs. Gage," I said. "There isn't anything to worry about."

And I hoped I was telling her the truth.

Seventeen

In the morning, first thing, I called the registrar's office at CCSF and asked the woman who answered if Nelson Mixer had recovered sufficiently—I didn't say from what—to get back to his classes this week. She told me he had. When I asked her about his schedule she said he had a free period from ten to eleven and that I might be able to find him then in his office in Batmale Hall.

Coffee, two more eggs, and a piece of dry toast passed for breakfast. But my bathroom scale said I'd lost another pound, which made four now, so I was able to choke the food down with less difficulty than usual.

I hung around drinking second and third cups of coffee, waiting for nine-thirty so I could call the DMV. Fletcher wasn't happy to hear from me again so soon, but when he got done bitching he agreed to run a computer list of all the Wakasas currently holding California driver's licenses. He'd have it for me, he said, in an hour or so.

I put my overcoat on and went downstairs and out into the new day. Some more rain had fallen during the night, but the sky was clearing now: scattered stratocumulus clouds, intermittent sunshine, a cold gusty December wind. The air had a clean, scrubbed smell, the way it does after a long period of rain. It also had a sharp, crystal clarity; out around the Cliff House you would not only be able to see the Farallone Islands thirty-two miles at sea but you'd be able to make out the exact contours of each of them.

Not hurrying, I started off toward Laguna Street, which was where I'd parked my car last night. I expected to encounter the white Ford somewhere nearby—I was looking for it, in fact—but when I spotted it, parked so that the two *kobun* could watch both my car and the entrance to my building, I felt myself getting angry all over again. God, they were persistent bastards; throw them off and they came right back with the fixated determination of cats. It gave me a paranoid hunted feeling.

Batmale Hall, on the City College campus, was a rectangular building of grayish stone, several stories high, built into a hillside so that if you entered it on the upper level you were already on the fourth floor. That was the way I came in, at twenty past ten. There wasn't any directory that I could see, so I stopped a couple of kids and asked them if they knew where Professor Mixer's office was. One of them did: fifth floor.

Rather than wait for an elevator, I walked up. Mixer's office was at the rear; I found it easily enough because it had his name framed alongside the door: NELSON MIXER—U.S. AND CALIFORNIA HISTORY. Below that were one listing of his office hours and another of his lecture hours in a different building, Cloud Hall.

The door was closed. I knocked on it, tried the knob, found it unlocked, and opened it and went inside. Mixer was there, alone, sitting behind a desk piled high with papers and books. Books were everywhere in the room—on the chairs and filing cabinets, stacked haphazardly on the floor, stuffed into shelves over two walls. Otherwise, the office was nondescript. Which made Mixer stand out even more than he would have in a crowd, because he was wearing a mauve-colored suit, a lemon-yellow shirt, and a mauve tie, all of which clashed violently with his wild red hair.

His first reaction to my entrance was an annoyed glare. Then he recognized me, and the look metamorphosed into one of persecution. His long scrawny neck seemed to extend out of his shirt collar like a fox's out of a burrow; his face immediately began to stain the same color as his hair.

"You!" he said. He dropped the pen he'd been scribbling with and bounced up to his feet. "What do you want this time? Why can't you leave me alone?"

"Take it easy, Mr. Mixer. All I want—"

"For God's sake!" he said. He came bounding out from behind the desk, dislodging one of the piles of his books in his hurry. The books made a series of thumping noises on the floor, but Mixer didn't notice; he was already at the door. He poked his head out into the hallway, then retracted it and shut the door and locked it. When he turned to face me he was panting a little. He looked as if he were on the run from a pack of hounds.

"Why don't you believe me?" he whispered.

"What?"

"I tell you, I never touched her."

"Touched who?"

"Clara. An intellectual relationship is all we had."

I was not going to play any more pattycake with him. I took a couple of steps in his direction and waggled a finger under his nose. He cowered back against the door, looking horrified, as if he thought I might be planning to turn him into fox soup.

"Listen, Mixer," I said, "we're going to have a talk—a nice, rational talk for a change. No more screwball stuff. You understand?"

"Screwball? Are you insinuating that I—?"

"Shut up," I said.

He shut up. Just like Artie Gage when Haruko spoke or gave him a look. It seemed I had finally discovered the secret of how to deal with the Mad Lecher.

I curled my lip at him, tough-guy fashion. Then I reached out and flicked some imaginary lint off the front of his mauve jacket. The sudden movement made him flinch, which was what I'd intended. Both Clara and her father, whoever *they* were, would have enjoyed this. Hell, I was beginning to enjoy it a little myself.

"All right, Mixer," I said. "Go on over to your desk and sit down. Don't say anything; just do what you're told."

He obeyed. And sat stiffly in his chair, looking up at me with bright, nervous eyes.

"The first thing we're going to get straight," I said, "is why I'm here. I'm not working for the father of any woman named Clara; I'm working for Haruko Gage. Is that clear?"

"Haruko who? Oh, the Fujita girl. Yes."

"So is it clear, or should I say it again?"

"No. I mean yes, it's clear."

"Good. Now do you remember why I'm working for Mrs. Gage?"

"Ah . . . no, I . . . no."

"I didn't think so. I'm working for her because she's been getting anonymous presents in the mail—pieces of jewelry—and I'm trying to find out who's sending them."

"Oh. Yes. Anonymous presents."

"Now you've got it. And I think the person responsible is connected to some Japanese guys named Tamura, Masaoka, and Hama. Those names ring any bells with you?"

He shook his head. His eyes were still bright and nervous, but there wasn't any guile in them. Still, he was a screwball—and so was the person who had murdered those three Japanese. Screwballs, as any psychiatrist will tell you, can be cunning as hell when it comes to concealing things about themselves.

I asked him, "How about Chiyoko Wakasa? Do you know that name?"

"Is she another of my former students? I'm not very good with names; I deal with so many in my classes . . ."

"Okay, forget it. What I want from you now is some information on the Japanese relocation camps during World War II."

That surprised him. Or seemed to. He said, "You do?"

"Yes, I do. You teach California history; you ought to know something about them."

"Of course I know something about them." Now he sounded indignant, as if I had impugned his credentials as a teacher. "I know quite a bit about them, as a matter of fact."

"Is that right?"

"Yes. I once wrote a paper on the wartime evacuation of Japanese-Americans. A fascinating study, from the historical point of view."

"Sure. Unless you happened to be in one of the camps."

"Oh, yes," he said. "Tragic. Very tragic. Families uprooted, stripped of their possessions, shunted off to live in dreary tar-paper barracks behind barbed-wire fences." He shook his head. "Tragic," he said again, and he seemed to mean it.

I started to say something, but Mixer wasn't finished yet. He seemed to be warming to the subject. "Politics, war-induced hyste-

ria, racism—those were the three principle reasons behind the decision to relocate. The idea that all the Nisei and Issei in California
were potential spies and saboteurs is ridiculous. Did the government
decide to imprison American citizens of German or Italian descent?
Of course not; *they* were white. Nor was there any mass evacuation
of people of Japanese ancestry in the Hawaiian Islands, even though
more of them lived there than here on the West Coast: 157,000 as
compared to 120,000. What the Hawaiians did was to round up
known dissidents and ship them to the mainland camps—a total of
less than a thousand, or a mere one percent of the adult Japanese
population. Were you aware of that?"

"No," I said, "I wasn't."

"A gross miscarriage of justice," Mixer said, and nodded his head
emphatically.

"How many camps were there altogether?"

"Ten. Two in California, two in Arizona, two in Arkansas, and
one each in Wyoming, Colorado, Idaho, and Utah."

"The one I'm interested in was a California camp—Tule Lake."

"The California camps were the worst," Mixer said. "Tule Lake
and Manzanar—woeful places. Barracks partitioned into one-room
apartments twenty by twenty-five feet, each one occupied by eight
to ten people. No furniture; just Army cots and bed ticking. Inadequate sanitation facilities, inadequate hospital facilities; insuffient
food in most camps. And the allowances the people were given
. . . my God! Eight dollars a month for unskilled labor, twelve dollars
for skilled labor, sixteen to nineteen dollars for professional work.
And even then, the people didn't start receiving their money until
the War Relocation Board took control of the camps in the summer
of 1942, three months after the first evacuation orders came out of
Washington."

Pretty grim stuff. I remembered feeling sympathy for the Japanese-Americans when it was happening; my family and a Nisei
family had been friendly in the Noe Valley district where I grew up.
But I'd forgotten about their plight as time passed, ignored the
suffering and the injustice. Too many others had forgotten and
ignored too, without any feeling of shame or culpability. It was only
in recent years that some effort at reparation had been made—too
little, too late, to too few of the survivors.

I said, "Tell me about Tule Lake. What kind of camp was it?"

"The worst of them," Mixer said. "Isolated, with its own irrigated farm land so that it was self-supporting; but there were sixteen thousand people jammed into it, an uneasy mix of Pacific Coast farm workers and their families and recalcitrants from other camps and from Hawaii. It was also the official 'Segregation Center,' where the small percentage of Issei who requested repatriation to Japan and Nisei who renounced their American citizenship were sent."

"It sounds pretty woeful, all right."

"Yes. Boredom, fear, distrust, suspicion, greed—those were the everyday elements of life at Tule Lake."

"Was there much crime, then?"

"My God, yes. Graft, theft, rape, assault, two murders. Not to mention countless disturbances. Members of the *Hokoku Seinen Dan*—young men who advocated renunciation and repatriation— used to blow bugles early in the morning and hold marches and generally terrorize the peaceful residents."

I remember old Charley Takeuchi telling me that Kazuo Hama had blown bugles before dawn. I asked Mixer, "Was it only the *Hokoku* members who blew horns?"

"No. Other young men did it too."

So Kazuo Hama may or may not have been a dissident during his stay at Tule Lake; ditto Simon Tamura and Sanjiro Masaoka. But even if they had been dissidents, I couldn't see any connection between that and their being killed forty years later; or between that and their jewelry being sent to Haruko Gage.

"Those two camp murders you mentioned," I said. "Were they both solved?"

"One was. The other, no."

"Who was the victim of the unsolved one?"

"The general manager of the camp cooperative, a man named . . . I believe it was Noma, Takeo Noma. He was stabbed to death. The theory at the time, which seems probable, is that he was killed because he was an *inu*."

"What's an *inu*?"

"Literally, the word means dog. In the camps it meant an informer, a cheat, a traitor. Noma was hated by nearly everyone at Tule Lake; they considered his death a blessing."

"There were no leads to who killed him?"

"Several leads. And several men were put into the stockade—the probable killers, in fact. But none was ever indicted; the evidence was too circumstantial."

"I don't suppose you remember the names of those men?"

"Not offhand. Do you want me to look them up?"

"If you can do it here and now."

He nodded, got out of his chair and went to one of the wall shelves and began rummaging through the books there. He picked one out and thumbed through it; put it back and found another and thumbed through that until he located the list of names. He read them off to me, close to a dozen of them.

No Hama. No Tamura. No Masaoka. No Wakasa. And no Fujita. Zip.

Mixer put the book away, adjusted his mauve jacket and his yellow shirt cuffs in a way that suggested a fox preening itself, and made a small production out of consulting his watch. "Is there anything else you want to know?" he said. "I have an eleven o'clock class."

"That should do it."

"Should I expect you to bother me again?"

"Why? Don't you like my company?"

"Frankly, no." The persecuted look came back into his eyes. "I'm a peaceful man. I hate violence."

"I don't remember getting violent with you."

"You would have if I hadn't told you what you wanted to know."

"Well, you know how it is with us private eyes," I said. "We like to talk tough and beat up on people once in a while. Just so we don't get rusty."

He looked at me as if he were afraid I might jump him after all. "I'm a peaceful man," he said again.

"Sure you are. A lover, not a fighter."

"I don't know what you mean by that."

"Yes you do." I moved over to the door and unlocked it and opened it up. "Tell Darlene her father's looking forward to those home movies you took the other day."

"What?" he said. "*What?*"

I went out and shut the door softly behind me.

* * * *

There were public telephone booths on the main floor of Batmale Hall, and I used one of them to look up the number of the Slim-Taper Shirt Company and then to dial it. Somebody at Slim-Taper went and got Eberhardt for me, but the three of us might have saved the effort it took. Jack Logan had been up to his ears in a drug-related triple homicide in Visitacion Valley, Eberhardt said, and not inclined to spend any time at all checking out either jewelry or deaths in Princeton and Petaluma. Besides, the Tamura killing was McFate's case—we should go talk to McFate.

Yeah.

I told Eberhardt I would see him later and rang off. It was all up to me now, like it or not.

Another call to the DMV. Fletcher had the list ready for me: eight Wakasas with California driver's licenses, none of them named Michio; three in the Bay Area, one in Fresno, one in Eureka, one in Vacaville, and two in Southern California. Of the three locals, two lived in Oakland and one in Palo Alto. I wrote down all the names and addresses, thanked Fletcher again, assured him I wouldn't bother him any more for a while, and rang off.

I still had two hours until my meeting with Haruko Gage, and as I crossed the campus I decided to go home and use the time to telephone Wakasas. But I changed my mind when I came out on Phelan Avenue and again confronted the white Ford and the two *kobun* sitting inside it. Enough was enough. The Wakasa telephoning would have to wait a while.

The time had come for me to deal with the Yakuza, one way or another.

Eighteen

The Kara Maru Restaurant was on China Basin Boulevard a block or so off Third Street, tucked up between Pier 52 and a marine salvage company. It had once been a small ocean-going freighter and

it still looked seaworthy; or it would have except for the canopied
gangplank that led up to it from the wharfside, the silk banner
proclaiming its name in English letters and Japanese ideographs, and
the big sign in front that said you could get lunch, dinner, and
cocktails every day except Sunday.

There was a parking area off to one side, mostly empty this early
in the day, and I put my car into one of the slots. The white Ford
stopped back on the street, alongside the long Pier 52 shed. When
I got out I could see the two of them through the Ford's windshield;
if they were surprised that I'd led them here, you couldn't tell it from
their actions or their expressions.

It was cold this close to the Bay, and cold inside the Kara Maru,
too, despite the unit heaters that had been mounted on the bulkheads. Cold and damp and a little musty, like an empty cargo hold
or a shore cottage that has been closed up for several months. Creaks
and groans from mooring hawsers and old caulked joints. A suggestion of movement underfoot, although the boat was tightly anchored
to the wharf to keep it steady and its customers from throwing up
on each other in bad weather. Teakwood tables and chairs, big
soft-cushioned ship's couches in the bar lounge and restaurant
booths, and lots of highly polished brass fittings—nautical clocks,
compasses, sextants, and the like—to complete the decor.

The lounge was off to the left as you came in; there wasn't
anybody in it except for a black-jacketed bartender. Straight ahead
was a kind of foyer with another black-jacketed Japanese holding
forth behind a podium thing built to resemble a ship's wheel housing. Behind him was the main dining room: thirty or forty tables,
half that many booths. Only two of the tables and one of the booths
were occupied at the moment.

I went ahead to the guy at the podium. He smiled and bowed and
said, "*Yoku irasshaimash'ta!* One for lunch, sir?"

"No," I said. "I'm here to see Mr. Okubo. Hisayuki Okubo."

The smile vanished and his face went blank; it was as if some part
of him had been switched off. He said in a flat voice, "Please wait
in the lounge, sir."

"Don't you want my name or anything?"

"Please wait in the lounge, sir."

So I went into the lounge and sat at the bar and ordered a plain tomato juice. Nothing happened until I was halfway through the drink; then a lump of a guy in a dark blue suit came in and approached me. He had no hair, not much in the way of ears, and eyes sunk so deep in heavy flesh that they were like holes poked in bread dough. The *sumo* wrestler type. The bouncer and bodyguard type.

He stopped next to my stool and said, "Yes, please?"

"I want to see Mr. Okubo."

"Your name, please?"

I had already gotten out one of my business cards; I handed it to him.

Without looking at the card he said, "Your purpose?"

"A personal matter."

"Your purpose, please?"

"Simon Tamura. Ken Yamasaki. The two men in the white Ford."

For all the reaction he gave that, I might have just recited my Christmas card list. He said, "Wait, please," and went away with my card.

I sat there for another ten minutes, finishing my tomato juice. More people came in—tourists, mostly, with a few business types sprinkled among them. None of the customers was Japanese.

The Lump came back finally and stopped where he had before and handed me back my card. "So sorry," he said. "It is not possible."

"You mean Mr. Okubo won't see me?"

"It is not possible. Good-bye, please." And he turned and lumbered off toward the foyer.

It made me angry; it made me *damned* angry. I got off the stool and went after him and caught up just as he was nearing a door amidships, at the rear of the foyer. I scooted around in front of him, blocked his way. He stopped and looked at me out of those sunken eyes—the kind of look that was supposed to make me shrivel up and crawl away. I gave it right back to him, letting him see my anger.

"I've got a message for Mr. Okubo," I said quietly. "Tell him that unless he agrees to see me, I'm going to start busting this place up. You know, destroy things—furniture, dishes, whatever I can lay my hands on. Maybe knock some of his people around a little too. One man can do a lot of damage in a few minutes. Then he'll have to call the police; too many witnesses for him to do anything else. There'll be newspaper reporters along when the cops get here, and I'll tell them why I did it. Simon Tamura, Ken Yamasaki, the two men in the white Ford. Plus everything else I know about the Yakuza and the Kara Maru. It'll be all over the papers tomorrow, he can bet on that. Should be great for business."

The Lump didn't react or move or speak.

"I know what you're thinking, pal," I said. "You're thinking you're a pretty big guy yourself and you and one or two of your friends can stop me before I do much damage. But don't count on it; I'm just as tough as you are. Tougher, because I'm mad as hell. Tell Mr. Okubo that too. Either he and I talk like gentlemen or you and I fight like animals."

He spent another few seconds absorbing all of that. Then some more customers came in and animated him again. He said, "Wait, please," and made a careful sidestep around me and disappeared through the amidships door.

I went over to lean against one of the bulkheads. What I'd said about busting the place up had been a bluff; I was too old for that kind of brawl, and it would not only land me in jail, it would get my license yanked all over again—for good this time. But Mr. Okubo didn't know any of that. He would either buy the bluff or he wouldn't, on its own merits. It all depended on what he thought of me and how much it mattered to him whether he gave me an audience or not.

I had to wait more than ten minutes this time, and I was wired pretty good when the Lump reappeared. He stood in the open doorway and beckoned to me: Okubo had bought the bluff. I moved over there and into a companionway, and the Lump let the door swing shut. But we didn't go anywhere just yet.

He said, "Weapons, please."

"I'm not carrying any weapons."

"You will please allow me to search."

"I don't think so," I said. I did not want him putting his hands on me. Instead I backed off a ways, in case he had any ideas of getting rough, and opened my jacket. He didn't move. So I took the jacket off, tossed it to him, watched him paw through it. Then I turned around in a slow circle so he could see that the only bulges on my body were made by fat deposits. "Satisfied?"

"Hai," he said. He let me have my jacket back and waited until I put it on. "This way, please."

We went down the companionway, made a left-hand-turn into another one. At the far end of the second one was a closed door. The Lump tapped on the door in a deferential way, reached down to open it, and then stood aside to let me go in first.

It was a big compartment outfitted as an office, with carpeting on the deck and Japanese woodblock prints on the bulkheads and a massive teak desk set between a pair of portholes that looked out over the Bay. Some overstuffed chairs were arranged on the left side; on the right side was an elaborate teak bar. The room was soundproofed: when the Lump shut the door you couldn't hear any of the restaurant sounds, or the cries of gulls outside.

There were two men in the compartment. One of them was standing next to the desk; the other was sitting stiffly in the nearest of the overstuffed chairs. I took the standing one to be Hisayuki Okubo. He was a good deal older, better dressed—a tan suit made out of silk, from the looks of it—and had an air of authority about him. Still, he wasn't such-a-much. Short, a little on the plump side, with bland features and slicked-down hair like a gangster in an old George Raft movie.

Nobody moved for a few seconds. Then the guy in the silk suit came over to me, bowed slightly, and introduced himself. Okubo, all right. The Yakuza godfather. Not such-a-much in most ways, maybe, but when you saw his eyes up close like this, you could tell what he was made of. They were as cold and flat and hard as steel boilerplate, and they made a lie of the politeness in his voice and his manner.

I said, "I'll make this short and sweet, Mr. Okubo; we've both got better things to do. I'm here to ask you to leave me alone, quit having me followed. I didn't have anything to do with Simon Tamura's murder, so there's nothing for you to find out. Besides, it's annoying and it makes me nervous and it's interfering with my work."

Okubo was silent. So were the Lump and the guy in the chair, who looked tense and worried. It was so quiet in there I could hear myself breathing.

"Well, Mr. Okubo?" I said finally.

"Tell me, please, what work it is you are presently engaged in."

I told him. What I didn't tell him was that there was some kind of connection between the Tamura homicide and Haruko Gage's secret admirer. I did not want to get into that with him unless I was forced to.

He said, "You went to Mr. Tamura's bathhouse to speak with Ken Yamasaki—correct?"

"That's right. Mrs. Gage gave me his name along with a number of others, all former boyfriends. I've been trying to talk to Yamasaki ever since, but he hasn't been around."

"Why do you wish to speak with him?"

"The same reason I went to the bathhouse. And also because it's his car those two boys of yours are using to follow me around. But then, you already know that."

"Yes," Okubo said, "now I do."

"How was that again?"

"Also, those two men are not 'my boys,' as you put it."

"Sorry; I didn't mean that as a racial slur. *Kobun,* then, or whatever it is you call them."

"No," he said.

"No? Then what are they?"

"Friends of Mr. Yamasaki's."

"Not Yakuza?"

"Friends of Mr. Yamasaki's," he repeated.

"I don't think I understand . . ."

"Would you still like to speak with him?"

"Yamasaki? Yeah, I would."

"Very well. You may." He turned and made a gesture toward the young guy in the chair. "This is Mr. Ken Yamasaki."

It surprised me. I hadn't paid much attention to the young guy; now, when I looked at him, I could see just how tense and worried he was. Afraid, too: the fear was in his eyes and in the faint sheen of perspiration on his forehead. He was pretty much as Haruko had described him to me—on the near side of thirty, slender in a way that was almost girlish, with ascetic features enhanced by thick, black-rimmed glasses.

"Well, well," I said. "You want to tell me about these friends of yours, Mr. Yamasaki?"

Yamasaki didn't answer. He didn't look at me either; his gaze was on his hands chafing together in his lap. But then Okubo said something to him in Japanese, sharp words that made the young guy's head snap up and the fear flare momentarily bright in his eyes.

"I asked them to follow you," he said to me. "Without Mr. Okubo's permission."

"Or my knowledge," Okubo said.

Now I understood. It had been a private matter all along: nothing much to do with the Yakuza, really, except that Yamasaki and his two friends were low-level members of the organization. Okubo hadn't known anything about it until I showed up a little while ago; that was why he'd refused to see me at first. But when I made my threat he'd hauled Yamasaki in—the kid had already been here for some reason that didn't matter—and got the truth out of him.

All of which meant that the Yakuza wasn't interested in me at all. Or hadn't been until now. There was no telling yet which way things were going to go, although I liked my chances of getting off the hook better than I liked Yamasaki's.

I asked, "Why did you have your friends follow me?"

"The police told me it was I you came to see at the bathhouse. I had no idea why and it concerned me. I wished to find out."

Damn McFate and his big mouth. "So you were the one they kept talking to on the CB radio?"

"Yes. I let them use my car and borrowed my girlfriend's; she also has a Citizen's Band. That permitted us to communicate."

"All you had to do," I said, "was come and talk to me face to face. I'd have told you why I wanted to see you—gladly. There wasn't any need for you to play games."

Yamasaki looked at his hands again. There was embarrassment mingled with his anxiety now, as if he realized that his blunder was stupid and inexcusable and he'd lost a lot of face because of it. "*Gomen nasai*," he said softly. I didn't need a translator to know that he was saying he was sorry, as much to himself as to Okubo and me.

I turned my attention to Okubo. "What happens now? I don't want any trouble with you people; all I want is to be left alone to do my job."

"An admirable wish."

"I think so."

"Tell me this: Would you actually have carried out your threat to damage our establishment?"

"No," I said. "That was just a ruse."

"Ah. Very ingenious."

"Was it? That depends."

"On what?"

"On whether or not I get my wish."

"Of course," Okubo said, as if he were surprised that I might think otherwise. "We, too, do not want any trouble; like you, we only desire to be left alone to do our work."

I nodded, feeling relieved now. "What about Mr. Yamasaki's two friends?"

"They will not bother you any longer. I have already seen to that —by house telephone, before you entered."

"And Mr. Yamasaki? What happens to him?"

Okubo didn't say anything. Nobody said anything.

I decided the smart thing for me to do was to shut up. If I tried to argue Yamasaki's case, it would only get Okubo down on me again. The Yakuza and its code of honor were nothing for a Caucasian to try mixing in. Besides, I doubted if they'd do anything terminal to him; he hadn't screwed up badly enough for that sort of punishment.

Pretty soon Okubo said something to the Lump in Japanese; then he bowed to me, and I bowed to him, and the Lump led me out into the companionway. The last I saw of Ken Yamasaki, he was sitting stiff-backed in his chair with the sweat glistening on his cheeks and the fear glistening in his eyes.

The Lump walked me through the now-crowded and noisy restaurant, all the way out to the gangplank. I went down without looking at him, across the wind-swept parking area to my car. There was no sign of the white Ford, not there on the waterfront and not anywhere on my way to Japantown.

Art Gage opened the Victorian's front door in answer to my ring and said, "Haruko's not back yet." He looked and sounded short-tempered; his eyes, under their blond brows, were hostile.

Don't mess with me, kid, I thought. Not today. "I'll wait inside. That is, if you don't mind."

"Why should I mind? Come on in."

He took me into the familiar junk-filled parlor, said he had work to do upstairs in the studio, and started out. I said, "Wait a second. Is it all right if I use your phone?"

"What for?"

"To make some calls on. That's what people generally use phones for, isn't it?"

He made a prissy, disgusted noise with his lips. "What the hell, go ahead," he said. "It doesn't matter what I say, anyway."

It would, I thought, if you had anything to say.

He went out of the room and I moved over to where the telephone sat on a wobbly-looking table with rails around the top. I glanced at my watch as I picked up the receiver. It was just one o'clock.

I made Information calls first, to get the numbers of the eight Wakasas living in California. Seven were listed; the one in Fresno either had an unlisted number or no phone at all. Then I called each of those seven, starting with the ones in Oakland and Palo Alto. I did all of it by direct-dialing; the Gages would have to pay message-unit and long-distance charges regardless of whether they were on the phone bill or on my expense list.

There was no answer at one of the Oakland numbers; the other one drew a blank—the woman I spoke to had never heard of Michio Wakasa or Chiyoko Wakasa. Another blank in Palo Alto. And another in Eureka. No answer at the Vacaville number. Two more blanks at the Wakasa households in Southern California. Five down, three to go.

By the time I finished the last of the calls, it was after one-thirty. And Haruko still hadn't come home.

I began to feel the same edginess I had last night when I couldn't get hold of her. I sat on one of the fake Victorian chairs. Got up pretty soon and paced for a while. Stopped pacing and called the Oakland and Vacaville numbers again, still without getting a response at either place. Sat some more. Paced some more. Went to the bay windows and stood staring out at the empty street, at a sky that was clouding up again, building more rain.

Two o'clock. No Haruko.

Two-fifteen.

No Haruko.

Gage came clumping downstairs, poked his head into the parlor, saw me alone and pacing again, and said, "Where's Haruko?"

"She hasn't come back yet."

"What?" He came over to where I was and scowled at me, as if her not being there was my fault. And maybe, damn it, it was. "She should have been back by now, even on the Muni. She said she'd be here by one o'clock at the latest, because you were coming."

"She took the bus, you say?"

"Yes. Parking is such a hassle downtown."

"Does she usually call if she's going to be late?"

"She always calls."

"Where was this nine o'clock meeting of hers?"

"On Post Street. Post and Mason."

"Somebody's office, or what?"

"The Sundler Agency."

"You have their number?"

"I can look it up."

He did that; and I called the Sundler Agency and asked a woman with a nasal voice if Haruko Gage was still there. The woman said no, she wasn't, and sounded surprised at the question. Mrs. Gage, she said, had left their offices before lunch, at about eleven-thirty.

I put the handset down and turned to Gage and repeated the information to him. He looked worried and upset now—but not half as worried and upset as I was.

"All this time," he said. "Where the hell could she be?"

Yeah, I thought grimly. Where the hell could she be?

Nineteen

I left the Gage house at a quarter to three. Haruko still hadn't shown up, and Art Gage was working himself into a manic state and getting on my nerves. He was the type who can't handle a crisis, who always starts to unravel at the first sign of one. If I'd told him what I suspected, he'd have probably broken down into gibbering hysterics. As it was, the only things I did tell him where that I was going out looking for her and that he should stay put.

But *where* was I going to go looking for her? If she'd been kidnapped by her psychotic admirer, and I couldn't see any other explanation, I still had no inkling of who he was. Or what lay behind his fixation with her—the reason he'd murdered three men. And the only lead I had at the moment were those three remaining Wakasas, the two that hadn't answered their phones and the one in Eureka who wasn't listed.

All the way downtown, I kept thinking: This is my fault. I should have gone to see her last night, as late as it was; I should have insisted then that she go away somewhere safe. The thought was pointless and counterproductive, but I couldn't get it out of my head. If anything happened to Haruko . . .

The only place I could think to go was the new office for a conference with Eberhardt and some more telephoning. When I came in he was hammering a nail into one of the walls, hanging my framed blowup of the *Black Mask* cover.

"Be with you in a second," he said. "Just let me get this up."

The phones had been installed—old-fashioned black ones, thank God. I crossed to the one on my desk and called the Gage house. Artie answered instantly. He wasn't happy to hear from me again so soon—he'd thought it might be Haruko calling—and I wasn't happy that she still hadn't turned up. I cut the conversation short so I wouldn't have to listen to him break down some more.

Eberhardt was finished with the poster and watching me as I put the handset down. He said, "What's going on? You look grim."

I told him what was going on.

"Christ," he said. "If you're right and she's snatched, it'll be this time tomorrow before the boys at the Hall can act on it. She won't be officially missing for twenty-four hours, not without an eyewitness or some other evidence of kidnapping."

"And meanwhile," I said, "she's out there God knows where at the mercy of a lunatic."

"Don't jump down *my* throat, paisan. It's a lousy deal, but it's not my fault."

"No," I said. "I keep thinking it's mine."

"Why? You couldn't have known he'd go after her so soon."

"I suspected he might. I told you that last night, remember?"

"Bull. This'd be a hell of a world if we could run it by hindsight. You wops are as bad as us Jews when it comes to shouldering guilt."

"Yeah," I said.

"So what're you planning to do?"

"Keep trying to get through to the rest of the Wakasas. Call some of her ex-boyfriends, see what that gets me. And if none of it pans out . . . hell, I don't know. Go get that white jade ring and drive up to Petaluma and see if Kazuo Hama's family can positively identify it. Maybe the cops up there will listen to me then. At least they can help me get a line on how the Wakasa woman died, if nothing else."

"You seem convinced she's the key," he said.

I nodded. "I've got a feeling that if I can find out the how and why of her death, I'll be able to put the rest of it together."

I turned back to the phone and dialed the Oakland and Vacaville numbers again. Still no answer at either one. The telephone installer had left a couple of brand-new directories; I opened the white pages to the number of the Shimata Art Gallery in Japantown.

Eberhardt said, "I'll go downstairs and get us some coffee. You look like you could use a cup."

I looked at my watch. Three-thirty. "Okay, Eb, thanks—but make it quick, will you? If I'm still drawing blanks in fifteen minutes, I'd better get out of here and on the road to Petaluma. The rush-hour traffic'll be bad enough as it is."

He hustled out and I called the Shimata number. A woman's voice answered; she said Kinji Shimata wasn't there and was not expected back today. She wouldn't tell me where I could find him. Maybe there was something in that, and maybe he was out playing golf or getting a tooth filled or any one of a hundred other mundane things.

I called Nelson Mixer's house. No answer. Still at CCSF, maybe, which meant I couldn't reach him by phone. But I called there anyway, on the chance that he might have left for the day and signed out at the registrar's office. But as far as the woman I spoke to was concerned, he was presently conducting his three o'clock lecture on nineteenth-century U.S. history.

Ogada's Nursery wasn't listed in the San Francisco directory; I got the number from San Mateo County Information. No answer. Which didn't have to mean anything either; Edgar and his father both might be out somewhere doing mundane things of their own.

I considered calling Ken Yamasaki's number and decided that would be an exercise in futility. Even if the Yakuza had let him go with nothing more than a slap on the wrist, he didn't figure to be the man I was after. The probable time of Haruko Gage's abduction was between eleven-thirty and twelve, after she left the Sundler Agency and before she was able to board a bus for home, and at that time Yamasaki had been sitting and sweating in Hisayuki Okubo's private compartment on the Kara Maru.

Frustration and a mounting sense of desperation made me try the unanswered Oakland number again, even though it had only been ten minutes since I'd last dialed it. But someone had come home in those ten minutes—a teenage girl from the sound of her voice, probably just in from school. She picked up on the fourth ring and said, "Hi. Andy?"

"No," I said, and identified myself and said it was urgent that I locate either a man named Michio Wakasa who had once worked as a gardener in Petaluma, or any of his relatives. Silence. I thought at first that it was because she was disappointed I was not someone named Andy, but that wasn't it at all. Pretty soon she said, "My grandfather's name was Michio. My dad's father. He died about ten years ago."

"Did he once live in Petaluma?"

"I think so."

My hand was tight around the receiver now; I could feel the tension in my bad arm and across my back. "Did he have a daughter named Chiyoko?"

Pause. "That was my aunt's name. How come you're asking all this stuff about my family?"

"It's complicated," I said, "and I don't have the time to explain it so it'll make sense to you. But I'm a detective and I'm trying to find someone—a lady who's in serious trouble."

"She's not in my family, is she? This lady?"

"No. You don't know her. Tell me about your Aunt Chiyoko."

"Well, I don't know much about her. She died before I was born. In Petaluma, I think."

"How did she die?"

"I don't know. Nobody in the family ever talks about it."

Damn! "When will your mother and father be home?"

"My father's out of town on business. My mother'll be home around six. She works in San Francisco."

"She does? Where?"

"Embarcadero Center."

"Where in the Embarcadero Center?"

"I don't know if I should tell you that . . ."

"Please, it's very important."

"Well . . . Carnaby's. That's a shop in Number Two."

"Thanks, honey," I said. "Thanks very much."

I was putting the receiver down when Eberhardt came back with the coffee. He read the look on my face and said, "You get something?"

"Looks that way. The name of Chiyoko Wakasa's sister-in-law and the place where she works—right here in the city." I took one of the styrofoam cups he was carrying, unlidded it, drank a slug of coffee, and then put the cup down on the desk and started for the door. "I'll call you if it leads anywhere definite."

"Luck, huh?"

"It's not me who needs it," I said. "It's Haruko Gage."

The Embarcadero Center is a four-block complex opposite the Ferry Building, and not far from my previous office on Drumm Street. It had been built progressively over the past several years— high-rise office buildings, with arcades on the lower two levels full of artwork and yellow crysanthemums and lots of shops and cafés. You could get from one block to another via covered and open-air areaways spanning the streets, but that wasn't how I entered Number Two. I parked illegally on its Sacramento Street side, because it was four-thirty and raining again and the streets were full of departing office workers and both curbside and garage parking were time-consuming chores, and I went in through the main ground-floor entrance.

Carnaby's, according to the lobby directory, was up on the first level. I took the escalator and found the shop easily enough. It was one of those places that sold package wrapping items, greeting cards,

papercraft, decorator candles that sort of thing; now, because it was
December, all the stuff was aimed at the Christmas trade. A music
tape was playing "Jingle Bells" when I came in. As tense as I was
right then, the holiday song grated on my nerves like a file screeching
on metal.

The store was moderately crowded with after-work shoppers, and
the three salesladies were busy. Only one of the three was Japanese
—a short, harried woman with graying hair and big pendant earrings
that danced every time she moved. She wasn't working the cash
register, which made it easier for me to coax her off to one side,
confirm that she was Mrs. Wakasa, and then explain to her who I
was and why I was there.

She didn't want to talk to me at first. She kept telling me she was
too busy, she couldn't take the time, her boss would fire her, but the
real reason was the topic itself; you could see the reluctance in her
eyes, and something else, too, that might have been a deeply in-
grained sense of familial disgrace. But I kept after her, repeating how
important it was, saying that the information might help save a
woman's life. And I got it out of her finally—in grudging little
chunks, without all the details, but everything I needed to know.

"Chiyoko died by her own hand," Mrs. Wakasa said.

"You mean she committed suicide?"

"Yes. Poison."

"Why?"

"She couldn't live with her shame."

"What shame?"

"The thing that happened to her at the camp."

"The Tule Lake camp, you mean?"

"Yes."

"What happened to her there?"

"She was . . . attacked."

"Raped? She was raped?"

"By three boys. Not long before the war ended."

"Who were the three boys?"

"She couldn't identify them; it was too dark. Another boy heard
her cries and chased them away, but it was too late."

"Do you know who that other boy was?"

"I don't remember his name."

"Did he know Chiyoko before the attack?"

"Yes. They were friends."

"Was she hurt? Physically, I mean."

"They . . . she could not have children."

"Is that part of the reason she killed herself?"

"Yes. She wanted children very badly."

"After she died, a man Kazuo Hama built a mausoleum for her to be buried in. Did you know that?"

"Yes."

"Do you know why he did it?"

"My husband's father had no money and Mr. Hama did."

"He was a friend of Chiyoko's, then?"

"He knew her in the camp, he said."

"But Mr. Hama wasn't the one who chased away the three rapists?"

"No."

That was all she had to tell me. But she also had one thing to show me—the last little quicksilver bead that put the whole thing together. I asked her if the family had kept any photographs of Chiyoko, and she said yes, she had one among other family photos in her purse, of her husband and Chiyoko taken just after they were released from Tule Lake, and she got her purse and showed it to me.

Chiyoko Wakasa and Haruko Gage looked enough alike to have been sisters.

Outside in the car, with the office workers and the rush-hour traffic streaming wetly around me, I sat remembering things.

I remembered a pickup truck with a bashed-in fender and a busted headlight. I remembered eyes that had the dull sheen of someone who had been burning a lot of midnight oil—or so I'd thought at the time. I remembered a son asking his father what had happened to some live seafoam and shooting-star miniatures, and thought that both those things could be types of roses. I remembered that same son telling me his mother had died this past summer and how rough her death had been on his father. I remembered that the Feast of the Lanterns had also taken place this past summer, and that it was a festival to commemorate the dead, and the names of those I'd been told were there.

And when I got done remembering these things, I was pretty sure

I knew who had murdered Simon Tamura and Sanjiro Masaoka and
Kazuo Hama, and who had sent those presents to Haruko Gage, and
who had almost surely abducted her this afternoon.

The nursery man—Edgar Ogada's father.

Twenty

It was dark and raining heavily when I got to the Ogada Nursery.
My headlights made a silver curtain of the rain as I came bouncing
in on the boggy access road; they shone in thin bright spatters off
the fiberglass walls of the greenhouses ahead. They also picked up
somebody at the door of the nearest greenhouse, the only lighted one
—somebody in a yellow slicker and rain hat.

The figure stood looking in my direction for a moment; then it
moved away from the greenhouse door and broke into a run. I took
the car over next to the potting shed, where its roof gave some
shelter from the driving rain. When I stepped out, the running
figure was only twenty yards away and slowing. Enough sidespill
from the headlights let me recognize him: Edgar Ogada.

He had slowed to a walk by the time he got to me. He stopped
and said, "Oh, it's you," and he sounded troubled. He looked troubled, too; his face was set in tight lines under the rain hat. "I thought
you were my uncle; I called him a while ago and he said he'd be right
over."

"Something wrong at the greenhouse?"

Edgar hesitated. Then, "I'm not sure. My father's got himself
locked inside. He won't let me in."

"Is he alone?"

"I don't know, I didn't hear anybody else. But with the rain, it's
hard to tell. He was in there when I got home a half hour ago."

"What's he doing?"

"Who knows? Whatever it is, he keeps talking to himself while
he's doing it. In Japanese."

"What is it he's saying?"

"Mixed-up stuff; I couldn't make out half of it. He . . . well, he's been acting weird lately. He works too hard."

"Weird in what way?"

"Talking to himself, running around until two or three in the morning, not filling orders, selling stuff that's already been sold. Or doing something with it; a lot of flowers have just disappeared."

"What kind of flowers?"

"Mostly roses—bushes and cut pieces."

"Edgar, was your father at the Tule Lake camp during World War II?"

"Tule Lake? Why do you want to know that?"

"Was he there?"

"Yeah. He was there."

"Was he married to your mother at the time?"

"No, he was only fourteen when they put him in that place— eighteen when the war ended. He met my mother in 1948."

"Did he ever speak of a woman he knew at Tule Lake named Chiyoko Wakasa?"

"Who? No. Chiyoko . . . that's Haruko's middle name . . ."

"Does your father also know that?"

"I guess so. I think I told him once, but—"

"All right, Edgar," I said. "Go on over to the house. Wait for your uncle there."

"Why should I? Say, what're you doing here, anyway? I don't—"

"*Now,* Edgar!"

I caught hold of his arm and turned him and gave him a push toward the house. I did not like getting rough with him, but there was no time for explanations; I'd wasted enough time already. And I wanted him out of the way when I went after his father.

I leaned into the car and shut off the engine and the headlamps and then got my flashlight. When I came out with it Edgar was standing twenty feet away in the rain, staring at me. But he wasn't making any moves in my direction. I quit looking at him, pivoted away from the car, and hurried across toward the lighted green-house.

If anything, the rain was coming down harder now, chill against my bare skin. Ahead, diagonally in front of the greenhouse door and some distance away from it, I could see Mr. Ogada's pickup truck.

Crumpled fender, broken headlight—some of the hard evidence the police would need, because the damage had to have happened when he ran down and killed Kazuo Hama.

I had enough facts now to make reasonable guesses at the rest. Tamura and Masaoka and Hama had been the three boys who'd raped Chiyoko Wakasa at Tule Lake. Mr. Ogada had been the boy who'd heard her cries and chased the others off—Chiyoko's friend, and probably in love with her. He hadn't done anything about the three rapists at the time; maybe he hadn't had a good look at them either in the dark, maybe he only suspected who they were. Or maybe he was afraid.

After the war he'd lost touch with Chiyoko. It was probable he hadn't even known of her death; or that it had taken place in the same town where Kazuo Hama lived, and that Hama had realized he was partly to blame and had tried to salve his guilty conscience by erecting a mausoleum for her remains. "There the wicked cease from troubling and the weary be at rest." I thought I understood that now, too. It hadn't just been meant for Chiyoko Wakasa; Hama had meant it for himself as well. She had been the weary—he had been the wicked whose troubling would also one day cease. And now, all these years later, it had.

So Mr. Ogada had met someone else and gotten married and had a son named Edgar and started a wholesale nursery business. And Hama and Tamura and Masaoka had gone on with *their* lives over the next thirty-five years. And Chiyoko Wakasa might have remained a fading memory for all of them if a number of things hadn't happened to freshen it, to slowly turn it into an obsession in Mr. Ogada's mind.

If Edgar hadn't met and started dating Haruko, who looked enough like Chiyoko to be her sister. If Mr. Ogada's wife hadn't died suddenly and left him lonely and depressed. If he hadn't somehow found out about Chiyoko's suicide, and why she had commited the act, and where she was buried. If he hadn't made up his mind to belatedly avenge her rape and her death. If he had not begun to confuse Chiyoko and Haruko in his mind, to believe that Haruko was some sort of reincarnation of the dead woman he had once loved.

Three murders. The presents to Haruko, the last three taken off the victims and offered not just as tokens of his love but as symbols of his vengeance. And now the kidnapping, because he must believe with all his heart that she really was Chiyoko, and he loved her, and he wanted her with him . . .

I passed between the pickup and the outer corner of the greenhouse, on my way to the door. The wind-hurled rain had begun to sting harder, and I realized that it was turning into hail. The pellets rattled like gravel against the fiberglass roof and walls of the greenhouse. With that sound and the shriek of the wind, there was no way I could hear anything that might be going on inside.

I paused at the door anyway, to find out if it was still locked. It was. Then I moved on to the adjoining greenhouse, stopped at that door and tried it. Also locked. But it was set into a wooden frame, which in turn was set into the sheet-metal front of the shed, and when I tugged on the knob the door moved loosely against its latch.

The hail kept rattling down; I could feel it smacking off my head, some of the pellets sliding inside the collar of my coat and cold along my neck. If I couldn't hear anything from out here, I thought, neither could Mr. Ogada hear anything from inside. I stepped back, set myself, and kicked the door hard and flat-footed next to the latch.

It was not much of a lock and it gave immediately and the door went slapping inward. I went in after it a couple of paces—and it was like entering Chiyoko Wakasa's mausoleum all over again. The smell was the same, only magnified: hundreds of flower blossoms sending out their cloyingly sweet fragrances, roses dominating. Funeral smell, death smell. Bile pumped into my throat. I had to swallow two or three times to keep from gagging.

I stood motionless, straining to see in the darkness. The fiberglass walls on my right showed some of the light in the adjoining greenhouse; but the panels were opaque, and the light made them gleam dully like a wall constructed of iridescent squares. I could make out the door over there, just barely, enough to tell that it was shut. But I could not see much between it and where I was—faint shapes and shadows, some of them bulky against the deeper black. I was going to have to use the flashlight if I wanted to get over there without breaking my neck or making enough noise to override the sound of the hail and alert Mr. Ogada.

I got out my handkerchief, used it first to wipe the wetness off my face, then covered the flash lens with it. When I switched the thing on, the diffused beam let me see some of the flowers: rose bushes in long rows, narcissus and daisies in clay pots, beds planted with a white-blooming bush I didn't recognize. The beam also showed me that the way to the connecting door was like an obstacle course; most of the available ground space was occupied with flowers, tools, hoses like coiled green snakes.

It took me three or four minutes to cover a distance of no more than forty yards. When I neared the connecting door I shut the flash off and eased up the rest of the way in darkness. The constant drum of hail had slackened now. I pressed my ear against the door, but I still couldn't hear anything. What was going *on* in there?

I got my hand around the door knob and rotated it slowly. It turned all the way, made a faint click; this one wasn't locked. All right. I held it that way for a few seconds, still listening, still hearing nothing. Then I took a breath and inched the door open until I could look past the edge of it.

At first all I could see was the back wall of that greenhouse, where the sprinkler valves were; benches close by strewn with potting soil in sacks and trays, benches farther away jammed with already potted plants. I opened the door wider, moving with it, looking the opposite way around its edge. And I saw them then, both of them, down along the same wall beyond a wheeled cart loaded with more plants.

He'd made a kind of bed for her, or maybe it was an altar: blankets draped over fifty-pound sacks of the potting soil. She was lying on it, supine but half on one side, dressed in a dirt-smudged white pullover and a dark skirt, one shoe off and one shoe on like My Son John in the nursery rhyme. Not moving, just lying there. From this distance I couldn't tell if she was alive or not.

Mr. Ogada was sitting on a rickety wooden chair near her, his head bowed as if in prayer, his eyes squeezed shut. He seemed shrunken, much older than he was. The naked roof lights made the skin of his face look waxy, like that of a corpse.

I stepped out around the door and started toward him, moving silently on the balls of my feet. But I'd only gone five feet when some sense or other warned him. His head jerked up, he saw me, and a single convulsive moment brought him onto his feet.

I stopped walking. He stared at me without recognition, said

something in Japanese. Then he realized who I was, or maybe just
that I was a Caucasian, and he said in English, "Why are you here?
I don't want you here. Go away."

"No, Mr. Ogada," I said. "I've come for Haruko."

"There is no one here by that name."

"Her name is Haruko."

"No. She is Chiyoku."

"I know Chiyoko," I said.

"How do you know her?"

"I know she's dead, Mr. Ogada."

"No," he said, and shook his head. "No."

"Is Haruko dead too? Did you hurt her?"

"Hurt her?" he said. "How could I harm such beauty? *They*
harmed her, not I." A string of words in Japanese. Then, "Chiyoko,
Chiyoko." His face was scrunched up now, as if he were about to
weep.

I took a tentative step; he didn't move. "Her name is Haruko
Gage," I said. "You kidnapped her, you brought her here against her
will. I have to take her back to her husband."

"No," and there was more force behind the word this time. "She
has no husband. She has only me."

"Chiyoko Wakasa is dead; *she* has no husband. Haruko Gage is
alive and married."

"No!"

Another step. And another. I was almost to the wheeled cart now,
less than thirty feet from where he stood blocking my way to
Haruko.

"Stop," he said. "You must not come any closer."

I had no choice. Step. Step.

"You must not go near her!" And he darted away to his left,
caught up a pair of shears propped against the inner wall, and came
toward me.

There was not going to be any reasoning with him; his eyes had
turned strange, feverish, with too much of the whites showing, and
he moved with a kind of plodding implacability. I moved, too, but
not to meet him; laterally to the nearest of the benches and slightly
behind it. Only ten feet separated us now. He held the shears in both
hands and cocked back under his right ear, so that the blades pointed
straight at my face.

He was less than five feet away when he made his lunge. But I was ready, my hands down on the bench, touching one of the soil trays, and as soon as he slashed at me with the shears I swept the tray up and hurled it at him.

It hit him on the collarbone and the soil showered upward over his face, blinding him momentarily, throwing him off-stride. Leaving him vulnerable. I was already around the bench, and I swung a forearm at the exposed side of his head, like a football player taking a cheap shot at an opponent. It caught him solidly on the cheekbone, knocked him off his feet and bounced him sideways into the wheeled cart. The cart buckled, spilling plants and more dirt; one of the clay pots struck him a glancing blow and opened a gash on the back of his skull. He thrashed a little, flopped over onto his side, then quit moving altogether. But he was alive; I could see a vein throbbing in his neck when I moved over to stand above him.

I stayed there for a few seconds, not liking myself much, even though I'd had to do what I'd done. I had not wanted to hurt him. He'd been hurt enough already; too many people had been hurt enough.

Haruko, I thought. I went to where she lay. Unconscious but breathing more or less normally; no marks on her anywhere that I could see. I wondered if he'd given her something, some sort of drug, but that didn't seem likely. I got down on one knee and chafed her hands and face, and pretty soon she began to stir. Fainted, I thought, that must be it. An overload of fear and out cold in self-defense.

I kept rubbing her hands and face. She groaned, and the muscles around her eyes rippled; the eyes popped open, blind with terror at first. Then they focused on me, recognized me. She made a choked sound and sat up and threw her arms around my neck, crying.

I held her for a time, until she started to quiet, then took a gentle grip on her arms and eased her away. She said thickly, "God, he . . . where is he? He . . ."

"Sshh, he can't hurt you now. He *didn't* hurt you, did he?"

"No. He . . . I thought he was going to. He's crazy . . . he kept saying things in Japanese, calling me Chiyoko, telling me he loved me . . ." She shuddered. More tears brimmed in her eyes.

I felt big and awkward and faintly sick at my stomach. I could still smell the cloying, funeral scent of the flowers in the other greenhouse, or thought I could. The damp earth, too. And the rain outside. And the sour-sweat stench of fear.

"He . . . he was waiting for me," she said, "when I started home this morning. He said Edgar wanted to see me. He was acting funny but I didn't . . . I never thought . . . I always liked him, he was always so nice to me. . . . He brought me here, in here, and locked the doors and started talking to me like that . . . Chiyoko, Chiyoko . . . he made me lie down here . . ." Another shudder. "I thought . . . I thought he was going to *rape* me. . . ."

Ah Jesus. "No," I said, "no, that's the last thing he would have done to you."

I got her on her feet, and when I turned her against me, bracing her body, she saw him lying there and made that little choking sound again. I looked at him too, in spite of myself, before I led her out of the greenhouse. Small and old and crumpled, with a thin trickle of blood on his head where the falling pot had struck him. A living corpse, with that waxy skin. Not even a man anymore.

Poor bastard, I thought, poor lost soul. Responsible for so many crimes, too many crimes—three murders, kidnapping, others. But were any of them really his fault? They would not have happened if it hadn't been for that other crime, the one he'd committed by accident so long ago. The crime that had put him in a prison and exposed him to the kind of violence such places breed. The crime that wasn't a crime, except in one of those lunatic times called war.

The crime of being born Japanese.

Twenty-one

Tuesday was another wet, dreary day. I spent most of it at the Hall of Justice and in the San Mateo County police station in Redwood City, making statements, answering questions. And finding out a few things, too.

Mr. Ogada had been taken to the county medical facility, where he was under treatment and under police guard. Edgar had gone with him last night; he was probably still there today. Haruko had as much as said she thought Edgar was irresponsible, but she'd been at least partially wrong. He had a fine sense of responsibility when it came to his father. He was a good kid; he'd get through this, and do a lot of growing up as a result of it.

After a night under heavy sedation, Mr. Ogada had been more or less coherent today and the cops had got enough out of him to pretty much substantiate how I'd pieced it together. He hadn't known Chiyoko Wakasa was dead until this past summer; it had been Simon Tamura who'd told him, and who'd also told him where she was buried, when they ran into each other at the Feast of the Lanterns festival. Tamura had known of her suicide because he and Kazuo Hama had still been in touch back in 1947.

The news that Chiyoko was dead, coupled with his seeing Haruko again that same day, had been the catalyst that had broken Mr. Ogada down. He'd gone to Petaluma and got into the mausoleum and begun filling it with flowers. He'd sent Haruko the first two presents, the diamond pendant and the sapphire earrings, thinking of her as Chiyoko. But in his rational moments he understood Chiyoko was dead, that the gang rape by Tamura and the other two had been the cause. He'd known all along that they were the ones who'd attacked Chiyoko that night in 1945, but at the time he'd been too afraid to snitch on them. Guilt began to gnaw at him, until the idea came that he must avenge her.

Tracking down his victims hadn't been difficult; he already knew where to find Tamura, and that Hama lived in Petaluma, and asking questions in the Japanese community had turned up Masaoka. Masaoka had been the first to die, struck on the head with a rock on Pillar Point. Then Kazuo Hama, run down by the pickup truck. Then, because Tamura had been the leader of the trio at Tule Lake, because Mr. Ogada hated Tamura the most, he'd gone to the bathhouse and hacked him to death with the samurai sword.

That should have been the end of it, but of course it wasn't. He'd avenged Chiyoko, he'd proven his love, but he still couldn't have her. On Sunday night he had gone to Cypress Hill Cemetery again, as he did periodically to bring new flowers, sneaking in over the back fence after the place was closed so the caretakers wouldn't see him, and he'd found me just emerging from the mausoleum; he couldn't have Chiyoko there either, not any more. But he *had* to have her;

it was an obsession now. And so on Monday morning he'd gone to Haruko's house, and seen her board the bus downtown, and followed the bus, and waited until she was finished with her appointment, and then talked her into coming with him to his nursery.

It was a pathetic story. Most crimes of passion and madness were pathetic when you stripped them down to their fundamentals, but that didn't make them any less painful or any less tragic for everyone concerned.

Haruko was back with Artie, and presumably they would lead a normal life from now on. The Hama family in Petaluma would have to try to live down what their father had done a long time ago in a place he should not have been; and sooner or later, they would. Edgar Ogada would take over the nursery. The Yakuza would install another head of its *mizu shobai* operations in San Francisco, if they hadn't already done so. I would share my new office with Eberhardt —for a while, at least—and there would be new jobs and the old ones would become memories, some good and some, like this one, very bad. Life goes on.

But that didn't make it easy to take on days like today. Wet, dreary days. Dull days. Painful days. Days where the highlight was watching Leo McFate eat a little crow. That had been nice, but it was a transitory thing: he'd digest the crow and pretty soon he'd forget he had ever eaten it and he'd be the same old Leo McFate. I had a hunch we would lock horns again one of these days.

I was feeling low when I got home at five-thirty. The only call on my answering machine made me feel even lower: Kerry, saying she'd be late, she had another meeting that was probably going to last until around seven. Why didn't I go ahead and have dinner without her.

Well, *damn*. I went into the kitchen, because the mention of dinner had set my stomach to growling in its empty, plaintive way, and opened the refrigerator and looked inside.

Eggs.

That was all that was in there—eggs.

I'd had eggs for breakfast, I'd had an omelette for lunch, I was sick of them. I was also sick of carrots and cucumbers and celery and lettuce and grapefruit and oranges and yogurt and cottage cheese and RyKrisp and tuna fish and hamburger patties, but mostly I was sick of eggs. I never wanted to eat another egg again. I never wanted to *see* another egg again.

I slammed the refrigerator door. And stood there for a time, hungry and frustrated. And went and got my coat and headed back out into the rain.

Kerry arrived a few minutes after eight. She rang the bell, but I didn't go and buzz her in; I knew she'd come up anyway and use her key. Besides, I was lying on the couch and I had no inclination to get up, not even for her.

Pretty soon I heard the key scrape in the lock and she came in. She called, "Hello? Anybody home?" and then she saw me and she said, "Oh, there you are. Why didn't you—?" Then she stopped talking, and stopped moving too, and stood with her mouth open a little, staring.

Not at me. What she was staring at was the stuff on the coffee table: the six empty Schlitz beer cans and the empty carton that had contained a jumbo deluxe Guido's House Special pizza with everything on it including anchovies, shrimps, and garlic olives.

I got the stare transferred to me soon enough, at which point it became an accusing glare. "Pizza and beer!" she said. "You broke your diet!"

I gave her a sheepish grin across the distended, the eggless, the satisfyingly *full* mound of my belly.

"Well?" she demanded. "Don't just lie there looking fat and complacent. Haven't you got anything to say?"

"Burp," I said.